THE MISADVENTURES OF ME AND MISS KITTY

The Misadventures of

Me and Miss Kitty

STACY FRANTZ

XULON ELITE

Xulon Press Elite
2301 Lucien Way #415
Maitland, FL 32751
407.339.4217
www.xulonpress.com

Paperback ISBN-13: 978-1-66287-019-4
Ebook ISBN-13: 978-1-66287-020-0

Have you ever wondered what life would be like on the road? Traveling around the country, seeing the sights? Sleeping in a different place every night? The thrill, the excitement, the adventure. That's not quite what it's like. Time passes with little to no notice out here. Days turn to weeks which turn to months before you even realize how much time has passed. Time is fluid, only picking up a load or delivering a load marks the passage of time on the road. I've been out here most of my life and what a life it's been.

My name is Tory and I am a truck driver. I travel with Miss Kitty who is a truck cat. What, did you think only dogs like riding in trucks? You might be surprised. Miss Kitty the truck kitty tends to find herself in a few precarious situations from time to time and I have to figure out what to do about it. This is our story; I hope you enjoy it.

By the way, next time you see a truck parked somewhere, look up in the windshield. Is there a pillow or a blanket up there? They probably have a pet on the truck. Keep watching for a minute, animals can usually sense someone looking into their home. Don't be surprised if you see a cat jump up into the window.

Chapter 1

FOUR IN THE MORNING the blasted alarm goes off, dang thing always goes off just when I'm finally getting comfortable. Grrr, I need my sleep. Who wants to get out of bed on a cold raining morning before the sun comes up? No one, that's who. Ugh! Alright, alright I'm up. Man, I really need my coffee right now. That's about the only way my brain wakes up. I really don't want to get out of bed. Alright, let me get the coffee going at least. While it's brewing, I had best get started on my pretrip. It's not like the truck broke down overnight while I slept. I'm not even awake yet, why do I have to get out here in the cold and rain to look at the tires and check the oil and all that wonderful stuff? I know, so I don't break down or cause an accident. Whatever. I'm not climbing under that muddy trailer to look at anything, if it's broke it's broke. Arg! What the heck? A flat tire? Do you think I have time for this? They can't make a tire that will last over a thousand miles? I have a delivery appointment and I can't be late so of course something would happen on a day like this. They looked fine last night, dang it. Just wonderful. Sigh. Better get on the phone and call breakdown so they can get someone out here quick. Is my coffee done yet? What a way to start the day.

I would have got up an hour earlier if I had known I'd have to deal with this today. Oh no! I forgot to turn the coffee pot on. Could anything else go wrong? Crap, I didn't say that out loud, did I? Sigh, well, another wonderful morning. Lord, help me not get upset, it's just a tire. I'll call breakdown.

I make the dreaded call.

"Morning, need to get a tire fixed first thing. Do you have anyone close by that can get right on this? I have a delivery that can't be late." I think I talk to breakdown more than my own family.

"Don't you always? I think we have someone close who is willing to get to you this early. You should have done a post trip so it could have been fixed last night." The guys in breakdown just love these calls so early in the morning before the shops open up. Not.

"I did my post trip and the tire was fine. Anyhow, that would be really great if you can get someone out here. Thanks."

"On it, I'll see how soon he can get out there."

Click. Short and to the point as usual.

Coffee! Just need coffee and things will be fine. Bless the one who invented coffee.

***

A little over half an hour later I hear: knock, knock. *"Miss, I need you to set the trailer brakes so I can get this tire fixed."* PHSHH as I pull the brake. *"Thanks, I'll be done in no time."* I just nod at him. I don't bother rolling down my window.

There's no reason for me to be rude, he's just doing his job. At least he was willing to get out of bed and come all the way out here, some of them wont. Actually, he got here pretty quick for a tire guy; I should be grateful. I guess I'll make one more cup of coffee and get my paperwork done.

I need a break. It's been 9 months since I've been home to see the family. Maybe I should try to get a load through to see how everyone is doing. That will give me a much-needed little break. I don't get through very often. It's not that I don't want to see everyone but who can afford to take time off work?

"All done. Just sign right here. Hope you have a great day. God bless you in your travels."

Sigh. "Thank you and God bless you for coming out so early on such a dreary morning to change that tire for me."

Nothing like feeling a little guilt first thing in the morning. This is a blessed day and I am thankful I didn't have a blowout while driving down the road. I could have been sitting alongside the road somewhere waiting for hours to get that tire fixed. Sometimes I forget how God looks out for me and protects me every day. Time to get rolling. I might be able to make it on time. I'm definitely asking for some hometime. I need a break.

Ring, Ring. "Hello."

"*Mom?*" Sob, sob.

"Babygirl? What's wrong? Are you ok?"

"*No.*" Sob, sob. "*Mom, you have to do something! They are going to put her to sleep! She is so sweet and so cute! You have to help her!*" Such desperate pleas from my daughter, this must be serious.

"What? Who Babygirl? What are you talking about?"

"*The kitty cat! They are going to put her to sleep! You love cats, you have to help her!*" Sob.

"What can I do? I'm over a thousand miles away and I don't have a house or any place to keep a cat."

"*She needs you mom! They are going to put her to sleep!*" Not good. She loves cats. What can I do?

Yeesh! "Well, I was just thinking about asking for a trip through there. Tell them not to put her to sleep till I get there. No promises but I'll see what I can do when I get there."

"*I knew you would help her! Thank you, mom. I love you so much! You will love her, I know it.*" I can almost feel the relief in her voice.

"I love you too Babygirl."

Click.

Well, geez, what am I going to do now? Oh boy, I must find a way to help that cat or my daughter will never forgive me. I've thought about getting a cat but I don't know how a cat would like the truck. Dogs like trucks. I guess I can try. I better get that hometime scheduled ASAP. Hopefully they won't put her to sleep before I can get there.

Lord, let the cat like living on a truck, that's the best I can do for it. I know the truck is small but let it be big enough. Thank you, Lord.

Chapter 2

IT TOOK ME OVER a week to get a load through home and in all that time no one came up with a name for the cat? At the shelter, they said she looks to be around 6 months old. Gray and white tabby with a bit of an attitude. At least they were able to get her spayed and give her all her shots before I arrived, I wouldn't be able to take her if they hadn't. I paid for them for all that and to keep her for me so she would be ready to go and she wouldn't be put to sleep before I could get to town.

I'm a little worried this might be a mistake. Well, it's time to go meet "Miss Kitty". That's what I've been calling her since no one came up with a name yet. I think she will like it.

"Mom! You made it! We have to go get Miss Kitty! Hurry!" She seems happy at least, maybe a bit too excited. Better than the desperate child who called her mom crying about a cat.

"Hello to you too Babygirl." She almost peels out of the parking lot. Looks like there's no time for pleasantries today.

"No time, we have to hurry. You are going to love her. Let's go!"

"Ok, let's go get Miss Kitty." This should be interesting. I hope she likes the truck because I can't bring her back once I leave. What have I gotten myself into now?

The lady at the shelter recognized my daughter's car and comes to greet us with a big smile.

"Oh, hi. I bet you are Tory. We have been waiting for you."

"Yes, thank you for getting the cat ready for me and keeping her here till I could get here."

"No problem. She is over there in that cage. We have to keep her separate from the other animals at all times so I'm sure she will be glad to get out."

"Did you have to keep her caged all the time? I thought you took the animals out occasionally to let them play."

"We usually try to do that but she doesn't like the other animals. Or people. Or anything. Your daughter said that it would be ok to keep her in the cage because she didn't want anything to happen to her until you could get here. She told us you love cats so much that you can tame the most feral of cats. You might find her to be quite the challenge. She does seem to like your daughter. Normally we have to let the feral cats live in the feral communities outside of town or put them to sleep. She didn't get along with the cats out there and doesn't get like the ones here either. There is just nothing we can do with cats like her."

Oh my goodness, I guess I have no choice. What have I gotten myself into? Well, I can't back out now, it would break my daughter's heart if they put her to sleep. There is a chance this will work out if she isn't too feral but what will she do on the truck? This is going to be interesting for sure.

"Hello Little Miss Kitty. Do you want to live with me and travel all over the country? I live in a big truck and go all over the place. You will see new sights every day. Would you like that?"

Purr, purr.

"She must like you, all she does is hiss and growl and scream at us. She seems to really like your daughter as well but no one else can get close to her."

Purr, purr.

"Mom, she loves you. I knew she would. You'll see, this will be great for both of you. You need her as much as she needs you. I'll go get the carrier." My anxious daughter runs to the car.

The minute she set the carrier down, Miss Kitty saw it.

"Hiss, growl, MEOW!"

"Umm, I don't think she likes the carrier. Let's just hold on to her till we get to the truck and see if she likes it there. She might not like it and we will have to find her a different home."

She calmed down in my lap but how is she going to respond to the truck, especially when the truck moves and I can't hold her?

She jumped out and right into the truck without hesitation as soon as I opened the car door.

"Look mom, she likes the truck, she is laying up there on top of the cabinet. Look, she likes jumping all over exploring everything. She loves it. She is going to make the best truck kitty ever!"

She does seem to like the truck. I don't know if she will feel the same when it starts moving. Guess I'll find out tomorrow. This will be a blessing or one very big mistake but for now, I have saved the kitty my daughter was so worried about so I'm a hero in her eyes. That's all that matters.

Dear Lord, help me figure this out. I am going to take the cat with me so keep her calm and let her adjust to traveling. Please keep us safe and don't let her get out or get lost along the way. Thank you, Lord.

Chapter 3

I HAVE TO LEAVE out because I am still under a load that has to get delivered on time. I wanted more time but this was the best I could do with such short notice. They did try to find a swap but the other loads wouldn't have allowed me to stay this long. I'll try to get back soon.

"Ok Babygirl, I have my groceries and I think I got everything I need for Miss Kitty. I love you and I'll try to get through again as soon as I can. Sorry I could only stay one night but I am under a load and have to get it to Virginia on time. Better tell Miss Kitty goodbye and remind her to be good on the truck."

"Ok mom. Be careful out there and I'm sure Miss Kitty will love you and keep you company so you don't have to be alone all the time."

Purr, purr.

A cat on the truck. That's something you don't see every day. That litter box better not stink. Where did she go? Is she hiding? She jumped out! Dang cat! Doesn't she know I just rescued her? Well, maybe she wants to stay here. Almost done getting the groceries put away, if she doesn't come back then it wasn't meant to be. *Thump!* What do you know? She came back before I drove off. At least she got back into the truck by herself. Now let's see how she likes it when it moves.

"Do you like it in the windshield Miss Kitty? I can put a bed up there for you but I have to warn you, it gets hot up there when the sun shines in."

Purr. She jumps into the seat.

"It got hot up there, didn't it? There ya go, that looks like a better spot. I'll have to get you a bed or pillow for that seat."

Purr.

"Where are you going now, don't jump up on top of things while we are moving, you might fall. Be careful, I'll have to move some things around for you but you will have to wait until we stop."

Purr.

Thank goodness she calmed down. I think she is handling this fairly well. She went right to sleep.

"Hey, are you just going to sleep all day? Don't you dare try keeping me up all night. Don't you want to see the scenery? Maybe I need to get you some more toys. Play or do something. I'm not staying up all night with you. I mean it. Are you listening?"

Purr.

***

Better stop here and get fuel, maybe grab a bite to eat. Should I go in the store to get her anything?

"Hey, where are you going? We only stopped to fuel. Don't you dare run off at a truck stop. Fine, if that's the way you want it. I'll leave the door open till I'm done fueling then I'm leaving. Do you hear me? I will leave you. Right here. At the truck stop." Dang cat, what was I thinking bringing a cat on the truck with me.

Thump. She jumped in as soon as I got in. I guess she doesn't want left here.

"Bout time you came back, I'm getting ready to leave. Did you have fun? Find anything interesting while you were out? I could have left you. Don't think I won't."

Purr.

Thank goodness she didn't run off. She is pretty cute laying there all curled up in the seat like that. Look at that little white spot on her side and it looks like she has the slightest hint of a white stripe down her back. Awe, I might actually enjoy having a kitty on the truck. It might not be so bad after all.

"Yes, fine, I'll roll the window down for you while we are stopped. Do you smell something interesting? What do you think about us being in a different place every time we stop? Do you like it? Would you rather have a home that doesn't move?"

"*Growl.*"

"So, you like the truck?"

Purr. Hmm, what a cat. I think she actually does like the truck. At least she has done well this far. I might have to call around to see if anyone would be willing to take her if she decides she doesn't like it. Nah, I think she will do just fine, she doesn't seem at all feral to me. Maybe she just didn't like the shelter.

***

"Really? We are stopping for the night. Must you smell the air every time we stop? Alright but no jumping out. I'm getting ready for bed, are you going to be up all night? I'm not leaving the window down all night. Awe, you want snuggles and pets? Ok, for a little bit. We have another long day of driving tomorrow; are you ok with that?"

Purr.

"I am a little surprised you didn't have any problems riding in the truck all day long."

Purr.

I have to admit, this was a good day. Miss Kitty seems to like the truck and even enjoys traveling. It is a little surprising that a cat would enjoy it so much. The traveling cat. I think every driver needs a cat. Wouldn't that be something. A kitty in the window everywhere you look.

Thank you, Lord, for allowing me to find a cat litter that hides the smell when she uses the cat box. That might have been a deal breaker. Thank you for keeping us safe today and for Miss Kitty to come back to the truck when she jumped out. I really don't know what I would have told my daughter. And one more thing Lord, please don't let her keep me up all night. We still have a long way to go and I used most of my free time stopping to pick her up. Thank you, Lord.

Chapter 4

GROAN, WHY DO THEY want deliveries at 2am? Why can't they just let us park on their property for the night so all they have to do is knock on the door in the morning? Then when they are ready for us to back in a dock, we are right there so they can unload the truck? It is bad enough getting up and driving so early but then we wait in a line of trucks to check in at guard shack just to get in the gate and have to check in again at the office only to be told to park until they are ready. Sigh, the life of a truck driver, so glamorous. Not. So much waiting. Ugh. At least we are here and we will be unloaded soon.

***

It is so beautiful here in Virginia. A whole lot of green everywhere. I bet Miss Kitty would love to get out and climb the trees here. I hope she knows how to get back down; those trees are pretty tall and there is no way I can climb up to rescue her. Maybe we can find some at a rest area that aren't so tall and she can get out for a while. I'll look for something later, maybe after we pick up the next load. I hope the day will be bright and sunny so we can sit outside for a while.

We finally get to the guard gate. All the guards start looking the same after a while. It doesn't matter if they are male, female, young, old or what color their hair, eyes or skin are, they all just seem to blend together. We see so many, everywhere we go, they all become just the gate guard.

"Little Miss Kitty, what are you doing? You can't check in. Quit sniffing the guard. I rolled your window down, go sniff the air on your side." Cats are definitely curious about everything.

"Awe, a cat on a truck. That's something you don't see every day. How does she do when you start driving? She doesn't seem afraid of the truck." The guard seems rather curious.

"She loves it, as you can see, she has beds everywhere so she can lay just about anywhere she wants and look out whenever she feels the need. Cats like to sleep a lot so I think that makes them perfect for the truck." I might spoil her just a little but I bet they see that with the dogs who come through here.

"I didn't think cats liked to travel."

"I don't know if all cats do, maybe she is special but she likes laying here and there just looking out at the world as it goes by." At least I think she does whether she agrees with me or not I don't know.

"Can I pet her?" Ugh, do I dare let her reach in here? Will Miss Kitty bite her? Should I let her try?

"I haven't had her very long and they told me she was a bit on the aggressive side so I would use a bit of caution, just in case." Should I let a stranger reach in? How is she going to react? Guess all I can do is give a warning and hope nothing bad happens.

"Look how cute. She is sniffing my hand. I think she likes me. Aaah! She tried to bite me. She seemed fine until I tried to pet her. Are you sure you should have her on the truck?"

Hmm, this might be a problem. This might be something I should worry about. Is she really feral like they said? She has never acted aggressive towards me in the slightest. Maybe I shouldn't let her over here on my side when I check in. Time to make it sound innocent.

"Sorry, she is a bit nervous with people reaching into the truck. She was just afraid you were going to try to take her away." Let's hope that's all it was.

"Awe, how sweet. It's ok baby, I would never try to steal you away. Aren't you just the cutest thing. She is so beautiful."

"Well, I better get in there so they can get the truck unloaded. You have a good day." Thank goodness she didn't actually bite or anything. I'm going to have to be more careful.

"Go on in and you two have a wonderful day."

Whew! That could have been a bad situation. What would they do to her if she bit someone? Would they put her down like they do to dogs when they bite? How am I supposed to handle something like this? This is something I had never really considered. Hmm. I'll just warn people she is a guard cat and tell them flat out they can't pet her from now on. That might work. I hope.

***

"Well, Miss Kitty, we got checked in and actually got into a dock right away. We are pretty lucky today. Care to explain what that was all about with the guard this morning?"

Meow.

"That is not an answer young lady. You can't bite anyone or they might take you away. You like your truck, don't you? You don't want them taking you back to the cage, do you?"

Meowowow!

"I didn't think so. You will have to be nice to the guards from now on. I will tell them not to pet you but you have to promise not to bite anyone. Understood?"

Meow. Purr.

I can't believe I'm having a conversation with a cat. They are very smart but do I really believe she understands what I'm saying? I actually hope she does, I really don't want to see anything bad happen to her. I think I like having her on the truck. She doesn't bother me while I'm driving and plays up front while I'm sleeping. She really does make an awesome truck cat. I need to thank my daughter for finding her for me. It's only been a few days but I'm enjoying having her with me. What did I do without a cat? It's already hard to imagine her not being here with me.

Lord, thank you for sending me a cat. You knew just the right one to send me, thank you. Thank you for keeping her from biting the guard, please keep her calm when we go into the customers so nothing bad happens.

Chapter 5

GET UP AND DRIVE, stop to fuel, grab lunch, drive, drive, drive. Stop for the night, get up and drive. Time passes and it all blurs together. How many days did this trip take? How long before we can take a day off? This is my life. So exciting, thrilling, action packed; no, not really, and it can get lonely. It gets tedious doing the same thing every day even if it is in different states. Time and distance stop meaning anything at all. What would I do without Miss Kitty keeping me company? How did I do this for so long without her with me? She has really made an impact in my life.

I finally found one toy Miss Kitty will play with. Yep, just one. The little fuzzy balls with the shiny things poking out all over. Nothing else I have bought interests her. The only way she will play with me is when we play fetch. Nothing and I mean nothing I have bought her even makes her curious. No feathers, none of the different kinds of balls, nothing with bells, not even catnip mice interest her. At least she wants me to throw her ball so she can go get it. I know she prefers to play with it outside the truck, but she still tries to run after it inside. Not a lot of room in here but she makes due. I wish I could give her something bigger but this is all I have to offer right now. Someday I might have a real house.

The first time she brought her ball to me I didn't know what she wanted. I threw it into the back where her toys belong and she brought it back to me. I threw it back there again and she brought it back again. That's how I discovered she liked playing fetch. She loves to throw it outside the truck herself so she has an excuse to go out to get it. Unfortunately, she forgets to bring them back in and I'm the one who has to fetch her ball.

What a way to start the day. We stayed at a rest area in Pennsylvania so Miss Kitty could play for a little while last night. All I did this morning was step out to do my pretrip and as I rounded the truck "Excuse me? What the heck?" Someone trying to get in my truck? Seriously?

Meowrl growl hiss growl yeowl meowrl.

Yikes, that is a mad cat. Wow, I have never really heard a man scream like that. I just thought it was a figure of speech for a man to scream like a girl. I can now assure you, it is not. I think he might just put an opera singer to shame. He hit a note so high I think it might be wise to check my windows to make sure they didn't crack. Dang, he sure can run fast. There is no way I'm chasing him. Run dude, keep running. Nope, I'm going to get back in the truck and let him run as far as he wants.

Sigh. Great, should I call the cops? Maybe an ambulance? I should call dispatch at least. Hmm. What to do. Coffee first. I need to wake up fully before I do anything.

***

Ring, ring. Great, here we go.

"Hello and good morning."

"*What did you do?*" Guess dispatch got the news already. Maybe I should have called them right away.

"Excuse me?"

"*We got a call bright and early this morning about you attacking another driver.*" They sound mad.

"Me? Me attack an innocent driver? Are you serious? Why would I do something like that?"

"*Tory, this is a very serious allegation, you need to take this seriously. Now, What Did You Do?*"

"I do take attempted hijacking seriously. I'm very serious. Can't you hear how serious I am?"

"*This is no light matter. The driver wants to file charges. What? What are you talking about hijacking?*"

"Gee, he must have called you as he was running away, I guess he just forgot to tell you he was trying to hijack my truck. How nice of him to call you. I hope you got his name or something to identify him."

"I don't understand what you are talking about. He mentioned something about accidentally mistaking your truck for his. That is no reason for you to attack another driver and hurt him bad enough to need to go the hospital. Why did you attack him for an innocent mistake like that."

"You think this was an accident? A mistake? Right. Miss Kitty didn't think it was an accident or a mistake when he attempted to climb into her truck uninvited. You know I leave the door open while we step out to do our pretrip. He saw the door open and decided to help himself. She stopped him. I know I should have called the cops right away and I would have called an ambulance for him when I rounded the truck and saw all the blood but he ran away so fast. I just figured he made it to the hospital before an ambulance would have been able to get here. I don't feel sorry for him in the slightest and Miss Kitty has proven herself to be quite the guard kitty."

"Tory, this could be a real problem. Is she rabid?"

"No, she is not rabid. She has all her shots. She was doing her job. She is a guard kitty just protecting her truck. I've told you that before."

"Well, according to the gentleman, he accidentally opened the door to the truck, he was just confused and thought it was his truck. He said he was attacked by a wild animal."

"Gentleman? Really? A wild animal? Tell me, what company does he work for?"

"What? What does that matter?"

"Because all the trucks around me are a dark color with no special design or markings and my truck is white with purple stripes and swirls that reflect beautifully in the dark when light hits them. I think it a bit strange he accidentally mistook my truck for his, don't you? There aren't any trucks that look anything like my truck around here. And by the way, my door was already open so why would he say he opened it? His story doesn't add up."

"We need to check into this a little further. You definitely should have reported this sooner. You need to be more careful."

Click.

That went well. Not. What the heck? They just assume I'm out here beating up other drivers? Thanks a lot for knowing or trusting me or anything else. You would think they would know me by now. All I am is Just a driver, that is all they ever see. Well, fine, all they are is a desk jockey. They had best not do anything to Miss Kitty. She was just doing her job. She is a great truck kitty and a guard kitty. Her job is to protect the truck. She does have quite the bite but I'm rather proud of her.

Miss Kitty knew something was wrong right away. She went after him like a guard dog would if someone was to break in to its house. Whatever her story is, I might never know but I do believe God sent her to me and I'm very grateful. I personally haven't been afraid to be on the road by myself but it sure feels good to know I have a protector watching the truck for me while I sleep or if I step out of the truck. Some women are afraid to be out here alone. I can't say I blame them but I have always felt God watches over me, protects me and keeps me safe so I have never felt afraid no matter where I had to go. I don't know if I feel safer with a cat but I do feel grateful to have Miss Kitty. She is definitely a wonderful truck kitty. Thank you, Lord, for such a precious gift.

Well, now that all that is over, I need to get rolling, driving through Ohio seems to take forever and I don't want to deal with all the morning commute traffic out here if I wait any longer. I think it's funny the guy called in to report ME because now they know who he is and can track him down. I wonder if they will arrest him? Did he think he was going to get money out of that? Hmph. They better not tell me that I have to pay for any of his hospital bills. That aint happening. I wonder if that restaurant is still open in Indiana? They have really good food. Next stop, Indiana.

Lord, thank you for protecting us and keeping the truck from being stolen with all our stuff inside. Thank you for always watching over us. Thank you so much for sending me a guard cat. Keep us safe as we travel today.

Chapter 6

T AP, TAP... T AP, TAP... Tap, tap, poke. Yikes! I'm up! What the heck? What's going on? That little fuzzy paw tapping a little tap on my leg was fine but those sharp pin pricks of her not so little claws and boom, I'm fully awake, sitting up and ready to take on whatever is out there.

Meow.

"What? Why did you wake me up?"

Meow.

"Seriously? What time is it? The alarm didn't even go off yet." What is she doing waking me up? *Meow.* What could she possibly want this early in the morning? *Meow.* Where is my phone? What time is it?

Four in the morning? Crap, I let the battery go dead on the phone, no wonder the alarm hasn't gone off. Apparently, I now have a backup alarm clock. I need coffee.

"I'm going to teach you to make the coffee before waking me up like that. You did a great job getting me up but if my heart is going to be racing then my brain needs something to help it catch up."

Meow.

"Fine, I'm up. Give me a second to start coffee. Yes, I'll open the door for you, you need to learn patience in the mornings. You aren't a dog, you don't have to go outside first thing."

Meowlow.

It's almost like she wants to check if it's safe for me before I go out and do my pretrip this morning. She does come out with me to do the pretrip every morning and thankfully she comes back in with me as soon as it's done. She might do a better pretrip than I do. She actually noticed a problem before I did the other day. She started batting at the airlines. I wasn't sure what she was up to but when I looked closer, I noticed the spring clip had broken. That would have been a ticket for sure and could have caused a lot of problems if the lines would have broken or gotten a hole by rubbing or got caught on something.

This load has been nothing but trouble since we picked it up in New Jersey. They didn't have all the product that was ordered so we waited for three hours for another truck to get in with the rest of the product. The loader punctured some of the product on one of the pallets and had to take the damaged box off and rearrange the pallet. At least he fixed it before we left, I've had quite a few that didn't and they try to hide it in the middle so no one sees it. Guess what? When I get to the receiver and they unload it, they know they can't blame the driver because the damage was in the middle. Duh. It still gets reported back to the shipper and they go back to see who loaded the truck.

It took over five hours to get this load so we are running short on time to get it to the receiver since the delivery appointment hasn't changed. We can't afford any extra delays. There have been too many already.

The attempted hijacking in Pennsylvania sure didn't help. Thankfully they caught the guy and no charges were brought on me or Miss Kitty. It didn't take them long to find him, he was waiting for the company to pay his hospital bill. Three little stiches were all he needed. Whimp. Bet he thinks twice about doing that again.

I know cats have a sense of time when it comes to food but Little Miss Kitty seems to have a sense of time when it comes to loads as well. We travel from coast to coast but she seems to know what time zone we are in. She makes sure I'm up at the right times to make my appointments. Is there such a thing as reincarnation? Maybe she was a truck driver in a previous life? I don't believe in all that but it sure makes me wonder how she knows things. It isn't an instinct that an animal would normally have. It's like she really knows what she is doing out here. If I could only teach her to drive. Maybe I would if she could reach the pedals. Wouldn't that be a sight to see.

Miss Kitty the truck kitty. That has a ring to it. I know it has only been a short time since I got her but it feels like she has been with me so much longer. We make a great team. If I would have known what a blessing a cat could be, I would have gotten one sooner. Do you think every cat adapts to the road like this? Maybe she is just really special. Unique in the cat world. Maybe God made her just right for me.

Sunny California. That's where we are heading. We have spent way too much time out East if you ask me. Miss Kitty might like California. I think she will like the smell of the ocean and that fishy smell. Why do so many people want to live there? The prices are outrageous and the crime is high. I don't see the appeal. I guess they think it's worth it because of the beaches and mild winters. Not me. I don't mind the mid or Northern part of California as long as I don't go South of Bakersfield, I'm happy. I take that back, I dread San Francisco. That is an area you don't want to be in with a truck. They have a lot of loads in and out but very few truck stops or parking not to mention so many roads that are not made for trucks.

The days so often go by without notice out here. I hate driving through Indianapolis. I guess I say that about all the major cities. At least it's not as bad as Chicago, that is a complete nightmare. I should make it through St. Louis and maybe to Springfield before I have to fuel. This is a long trip. Looks like I'll be staying in misery for the night lol, ok, Missouri. It's about the same thing after all the dang hills on I-44. Up and down, feels like you're on a rollercoaster. I love all the caves out here. I wonder how Miss Kitty will like it when we have to drive into the caves? It's not very often but we do pick up or deliver in the caves. They aren't just in Missouri but those are the ones we get most of our loads from. That should be interesting for her. What will she smell down in the caves?

Hey, my cousin lives here in Tulsa, bet she would like to meet Miss Kitty. Shoot, maybe next time, we can't have any more delays on this load. We are only about half way there. I'll wave as I pass through.

The wind was so bad across I-40, it almost blew us over in Amarillo. Thank goodness it died down coming into New Mexico. I would have stopped at the casinos to eat but I don't know if any of their restaurants are open yet. I'm not much of a gambler but casinos usually have a good buffet.

The rain in Flagstaff didn't slow us down too much. Still good for on time delivery. This is a long trip but the pay is good. Miss Kitty has been fascinated by so many things but I haven't had the time to let her get out and explore. I really am going to have to make time for her. She gets bored on the truck too.

We made it to the closest truck stop to the receiver and it's still 90 miles away. I'm sure I'm going to have a lot of traffic in the morning, better leave about 4 hours before the appointment time if I want to get it there on time. Traffic is horrible in the mornings around the Los Angeles area. From the coast out to about Riverside you need to double if not triple the time it would normally take to drive there.

"Good morning, I have a delivery."

The guard sits at his desk ignoring me. His window is open. Like he didn't see or hear me just pull up. If nothing else he would hear me set the brakes right at his window. The only guards that ever stand out are the really bad ones or the really good ones. This doesn't look like he's going to be a good one. Sigh.

"*What time is your appointment?*" He sounds rather rude. Whatever.

"Seven this morning."

"*You aren't on the schedule for today.*" Is he serious? I just drove all the way across the country to get here, he better not play this game with me. It's been a long frustrating run.

"Excuse me? Can you double check that?"

"*You have a cat? Who travels with a cat? I don't think they allow cats here.*" What, he doesn't like cats? How surprising, bet they don't like him either.

"I just saw a dog in the truck that was leaving as I pulled in. You don't have any signs posted about not allowing pets. Are you going to refuse the load because of a pet on the truck?"

"*We allow pets but I don't think we allow cats.*" What? Why do people like him take a job at a truck gate if they don't like dealing with truck drivers?

He is going to make this difficult I can tell. Why would the company hire a guy like him to work at a truck gate?

Meow.

"Get that thing away from the window, it better not jump out, we don't want stray animals running around out here." He definitely doesn't like cats. Surely, he won't refuse to let me in the gate for that.

"She just wants to sniff you and know why you are holding us up at the gate."

"I told you; I don't think we allow cats in here." Liar. We might have a problem. As if this whole trip hasn't had enough of them already.

"You might want to double check that when you check on the delivery appointment. Please." Just be polite, we don't want any issues with this customer.

"Fine but you keep that cat in the truck." Right, like she wants to get out and be anywhere around him.

"No problem." He sure stomped back into his office. Reminds me of a child not getting his way.

Meow.

"It's ok Miss Kitty, he might not like cats but they won't refuse the load over something like that. Not everyone likes cats."

Meow.

"Sorry, we don't have you on the schedule. You will have to call to make an appointment."

"Can I pull in and park for a minute while I call my dispatcher to find out what is going on and what they want me to do about this?"

"No parking inside unless you have an appointment." We have a problem. Wonder who is going to get the blame for this? Jerk! I bet he didn't even check. I know we have an appointment and it is this morning so this is most likely all just due to his prejudice.

"Is there a truck stop nearby?"

"Why would I know where any of the truck stops are? You are going to have to get off this property. I don't care where you park, you just can't park here."

I hate coming to California. They are a major trucking state but have very few truck stops or places a truck can park especially in Southern Cal. How wonderful. The miles are good on a load like this and when you are paid by the mile it sounds like such a nice run but problems like this load has had makes me wonder if a local job might be better. You have the same customers all the time and know exactly where you are going. No refusals, no appointment needed, they are waiting for you so they get you unloaded right away and they need you to come back so they are a lot friendlier.

I just don't like the same routine all the time. I don't like always going to the same places and seeing the same faces day after day. I like the long drives across the country. I get up when I want, stop when I want and go to bed when I want. All I have to worry about is picking the load up on time and delivering it on time and the rest, I choose what and how I want to run. I choose the roads I take and the stops I make. That is what I like about being out here.

Look at that, I think I can get into that parking lot. I hope I can get back out again. Maybe I can drop the load somewhere for another driver to deliver. Then I would be able to just go pick up another load and get far, far away from California. Sounds good to me. Let's see what dispatch has to say about this. Aren't they going to be thrilled to get this call?

I make the call.

"*Why aren't you at the receiver?*"

"Good morning to you too. I was at the receiver. I already checked in or tried to. They said I don't have an appointment for today and I had to leave."

"*You shouldn't have left; you should have called me immediately.*"

"I was blocking the gate and I did ask if I could pull in to call you. The guard refused to let me stay on the property. Besides, I'm just down the road a bit."

"*I see where you are, your truck is pinging 7 miles from the receiver. You have to get back over there to the customer. You need to deliver that load this morning; we have you a load to New York this afternoon. It needs picked up before three, that's when they all go home, so make sure you are there before they leave or you won't get that load. Do you want stuck in California?*"

24

Of course, dispatch would ping my truck to see where it shows me at on the map, the computer must show me late for my appointment.

"No, I definitely don't want to get stuck here but like I said, they won't let me in without an appointment and they said I don't have one. You want to call to verify the appointment? Maybe they will work with you because you aren't setting at the gate. You can explain to me why they don't want me to bring my cat in as well."

"*What? They don't have any pet restrictions listed. Are they just keeping you out because of the cat?*"

"Wish I knew, that was my thoughts. The guard didn't want a cat in their yard. I'll leave it up to you to figure out the details. I can't go back up to the gate until you find out what's going on with the appointment so, please call me back when you know something."

"*Fine, I'll call you right back. You need to get over there now.*"

Click.

I can't go park in the middle of the road. If I had known this load was going to be such a pain in the backside, I would have refused it. Oh well, whatcha gonna do when you already ran the load all the way across the country? Sit and wait. Again. That's what you do.

Meow. Scratch, scratch. Meow.

"Really? You want out here? I think you had best stay in here for now. We might have to leave any second so I don't want you out."

Meow. Scratch, scratch. Meow.

"Fine, quit scratching the door up. I'll open it so you can look out but don't get out or run off. I do not want you out there around all the cars or near the road."

Meow.

Ring, ring. That was quick.

"What's the verdict?"

"*Get over there immediately! They said if you aren't there in the next ten minutes, they can't get you in until next week. Go. Go right now!*"

"Geez, it's not my fault I'm not there right now. They don't have a problem with my cat?"

"*They just said you have ten minutes or they won't unload you, didn't say anything about not allowing the cat.*"

"Leaving now. Thanks."

Click.

Where is Miss Kitty, she was just sitting in the floorboard looking out. Did she go outside?

"Miss Kitty? Little Miss Kitty. Where are you? We don't have time for games. Miss Kitty? I am not getting stuck in California, get back in the truck. Now. Where are you? I have to leave."

What am I going to do? I don't want to leave her, I'm kind of attached to the furball. I cannot miss this delivery. I refuse to be stuck in California. Lord, what do I do? I have to leave immediately. I'm going to have to get the load back over there. Maybe I can find her after I'm unloaded. I will come right back over here. Let her be waiting and ready for me please, Lord. I better find her, I'm going to be headed to New York this afternoon. God, forgive me but I have to leave her for now. I have to get this dagnabbed load delivered. I will be back. Get moving. Dagnabbed it!

The guard looks up and sees me. This time he at least acknowledges me being there.

"*Back again? Do you have an appointment? Where is that cat?*" He has a mean looking sneer on his face. What's he going to do? Search the truck for the cat? Geez!

"I was told I needed to get back here immediately that the guard at the gate never should have sent me away because they have been waiting on this load. Is that true? I think you need to actually call this time and you can let them know I was here before but you sent me away."

"*Whatever. I'll check again but I don't see you on the schedule. You can't come in if you're not on the schedule as I told you before.*"

He looks mad. Looks like I am on the schedule.

"*They said to get in door four or they aren't going to accept the load since you are late.*"

"Did you forget to tell them I was here on time but you sent me away? Never mind, I'll inform them when I take the bills inside and check in at the office. I'm sure they will understand why I'm late."

He looks double mad now. Hey, it's not my fault. What did he have against me anyhow? I didn't do anything to him. He might be the one who gets in trouble over this. Oh well, let's get this load in the door. If they hurry, I'll have time to go back and see if I can find Miss Kitty before I have to get the load. I don't want to get too far down the road without at least trying to find her. I better find her; I don't want to lose my kitty. Hurry up, wait, don't be late. Oh, the joys of trucking.

Finally! I have been so worried something bad would happen to Miss Kitty. I know I shouldn't have gone off and left her, she is so much more important than a load but I just didn't know what else to do. They wouldn't have unloaded the truck if I hadn't gotten there right then. Maybe if I can get parked here and open up the door she will come back home. This better not become a habit. I can't always go back to look for her.

"Miss Kitty? Little Miss Kitty. Where are you?" *Thump!*

Meow, purr.

"Thank goodness! I was so worried about you. Why did you jump out and why didn't you get back in truck before I had to leave? You better not do that to me again. What if I couldn't come back?"

Purr, purr.

"Rubbing against me is not an apology. You really had me scared. Let's not do that again, ok?"

Meow.

Thank you, Lord, for bringing her back to me. I don't think I could have left California without her. Forgive me for leaving her. I need her with me. She has been such a blessing in so many ways.

How do other drivers handle something like this? I can't be the only one to have to make a choice like that. Do they leave their beloved pet? Do they miss an appointment to search for them? What do they do? If they have to leave them behind, do they go back for them? I know they have to look for them. Their pet has to be a priority but do they lose their job over something like this? What do they do? How do they do it? Thankfully I got Miss Kitty back but what if she hadn't come back? Would I have left California without her? Would I have given up on her? How long can you search before you are forced to give up and get rolling?

The thought of other beloved pets out there searching for their mom or dad and not finding them breaks my heart. The driver who had to leave them behind must be suffering horribly. I hope there are good people out there who find those animals and take good care of them.

Lord, help everyone of the pets who had to be left behind for whatever reason find a loving home or somehow find their way back to the one who lost them. Don't abandon them and don't let them starve or come to harm. Please be with all the lost pets out there. Thank you, Lord.

Chapter 7

~~

"AGAIN? DO YOU HAVE to smell everything all the time? Does it smell different here?" I wish I knew what she was thinking. "Are you chittering at the birds or with the birds? Do you think they understand you?" She loves chittering at them when the window is down but it's a whole different story when she is out exploring and they come land by her. She has to have her window down to talk to them and smell them before she gets outside.

***

"Should we get out for a few and stretch our legs? I think I might need a jacket, it's just a little too cool for me. You have a fur coat; you should be just fine."

What the heck? Why in the world would she go flying back into the truck, as if she had wings, right after we got out? Ahh, the crows and seagulls. I understand, they are big and can carry her off. I've heard that sometimes they do carry off small animals, I don't blame her for being afraid. Owls do too, or at least I have read they do. Thankfully it's not dark, I don't think owls hunt in the daytime. I guess I need to watch out for the big birds, I don't want anything carrying her off.

"I guess people who stop here must feed the birds. I think they will leave us alone if we don't feed them. Are you still scared? I need to remember you are just a little kitty." That was so funny, Miss Kitty's hair stood on end and she turned into a fluff ball right before she ran into the truck. Good thing I left the door open for her or she might have run right through it making her own cat door. I can't help but laugh at her. I think she is a bit offended

29

that I had the audacity to laugh and that is quite funny to me also. How long has it been since I laughed out loud? It sure brightened my day even if it did insult her.

Too bad we didn't have a little more time, it was rather pretty there with the mountains all around. They were colored pink and yellow. If it hadn't been so chilly, we might have stayed just a little longer.

***

Driving, driving, driving seems like that's all we do. Yes, we do get out for little breaks but we have to put in a full day of driving or we will never get to where we have to be. Let's drive some more.

Ring, ring.

"Hey, what's up?" It's Sasha, a friend of mine that I haven't seen in a while.

"You said you're heading to New York, right?"

"Yep, heading up to Albany. I'm on I-71 right now. Where are you heading?"

"I picked up a load in Cleveland and am heading South to Nashville. What route are you taking? We might cross paths somewhere along the way." I might get to visit, cool.

"I'm actually not too far away from you, we might be able to meet at the TA over by Lodi, what town is it? Seville? Are you running through there?"

"That works, I can be there in about an hour."

"It might take me just a bit longer, can you wait?"

"I'll land there for the night."

"I guess we might both be stopping there for the night, that works out pretty good with my drive hours for the day. That gives us a little time to catch up."

"Good deal, see ya in a few."

Click.

"Hey, Miss Kitty, do you want to meet a friend of mine tonight? What do you think about meeting a little doggie?" Most of the time one of us is in a hurry to get a load picked up or delivered so we don't have time to stop but it's still nice to run past someone you know on occasion. These new drivers out here want to be home every other week so they don't care about having friends here on the road or stopping to grab a bite just to visit.

"Tonight, we are going to be able to stop at the same place, so we can grab dinner and visit for a bit. Does that sound fun? I guess not so much for you, you will have to stay in the truck but if you want, she can leave her little doggy over here with you to keep you company."

**

So many of my friends are dog people. Everyone seems to want a dog in their truck. My friend Sasha recently got a little poodle something mix. She calls him "Poochie" but I think his name is Eric. Who names a dog Eric? I guess that's why she calls him Poochie. Poochie loves cats. Turns out little dogs can jump up on things almost like a cat. On the dash, across the tops of the seats, onto the bed and all over the truck they ran. Miss Kitty finally found a place he couldn't or wouldn't jump to so she stayed up on top of the cabinets till we could get Poochie out of the truck. Miss Kitty was not impressed in the slightest and wouldn't come talk to the horrible person who brought a dog into her home.

"*You should get your cat out of the truck more. It can't be good for a cat couped up in the truck all the time.*"

"I do let her out. She even gets to explore things every now and then. She does my pretrip with me every morning. She doesn't have to go outside all the time like a dog."

"*I'm surprised she doesn't run off. You should train her on a leash so you can take her for walks.*"

"I have thought about training her to walk on a leash. Maybe I'll give it a shot. I think I bought one but I haven't tried to train her yet. Maybe I can do that tomorrow when we stop for a break."

"*Alright, I need to get to my truck and get some rest. Be safe out there. Maybe we will run into each other again before Christmas.*"

"That's still a ways out. Keep in touch, we might try for Thanksgiving this year. Be safe."

Maybe she is right, I should train Miss Kitty on the leash so I can walk her around more. I have seen videos on cats trained to walk on a leash and they do fine. Tomorrow should be a short day of driving; we are almost out of hours and there is no way I'm getting a ticket for an hours of service violation. Hours of service just means the hours we are allowed to drive in a day. You actually get a ticket and can be put out of service meaning you can't drive anymore that day just for driving longer than you are allowed for the day.

There are so many rules you have to know and follow if you want to drive out here. Most people don't understand just how much a driver has to learn and know just to keep their job. There is so much more to it than just driving around all the time. The rules change quite often so you always have to be aware of what they are and the changes they make.

We should have time to start her first lesson when we stop for our lunch break. Even if we stop for over our half hour break, we should be able to get the load there on time and it will give Miss Kitty a chance to get out of the truck for a little while. I do feel bad that she has to stay in such a small space so much of the time. Dogs don't seem to mind it much but they get to stop to get out and go potty a lot. I'll try to find a rest area with lots of open space and not too much traffic so we can see how she likes the leash.

I should buy her a reflective collar so they can see her better if she is out at night. I think they have a leash to match. That should keep her safer when she does the pretrips in the morning before the sun is up. Not that she goes far from the truck but she is so small they might not see her.

Lord, thank you for giving us friends to meet with up along the way so we don't get too lonely out here. Thank you for working out our route just right so we had time to meet up and visit not just a quick bite and away we go. Thank you for caring about us, keeping us safe and giving us time for friendships with other people as we go all across the country and back. Thank you, Lord.

Chapter 8

"WHAT ARE YOU DOING Miss Kitty?" This looks a lot easier when you see it on Facebook or those you tube videos. "Stand up. You are not paralyzed. You do not need an audience." I now know Miss Kitty is a total diva. So far, I've tried picking her up, tried pulling her along, tried everything I could think of and she just flops. That is until some people came walking by. She sat up straight with her head held high and actually posed for them. I'm serious. She posed like she was a fashion model. She even took a few steps like she was on a runway but the minute they were out of sight, she flopped again. If you have never seen a cat flop, you need to. All their muscles go limp and they act like they have no bones. This might take a lot more training than I thought. After an hour of trying to train her with the leash, I finally admit that I might need a lot more time and possibly some help.

This is a great day. We are having fun just laying here soaking in the sun. It's not too hot, not too cold, the sky is blue, no clouds blocking the sun, it's just what we needed. Lord, thank you for giving us the perfect day to get out of the truck for a while. Thank you for the beauty all around and the peaceful spot that has allowed us to relax and the trees that give just the right amount of shade. I think they cut the grass just before we got here, it smells so fresh and clean. Wow, look at those flowers. So many beautiful colors. This is great. Thank you for this, Lord.

We will have to work on the leash thing more but she did rather well for her first time. It might take a while for her to get the hang of it but she is very smart and if she can do it for attention and show off, she can learn to do it for fun. It will give her more freedom when we are able to go for walks away from the truck. I think she will enjoy that.

I just love having the rare short days of driving or the forced 34-hour resets when I'm completely out of hours. I get to relax and do some things that are not all truck related. Watch movies, get out and explore, do some shopping or even just do laundry and get things cleaned up. Just having time to accomplish something or maybe do nothing at all.

"Time to get things cleaned up on the truck Miss Kitty. You have too many balls running around."

Meow.

"Hey, get back here, do not, I repeat, do not chase that squirrel. Get down from there. You're getting too high up in that tree. Don't you dare say you can't get down. Miss Kitty! Get down here now."

Meow.

I think I need to find a way to put a cat tree in the truck, she really likes to climb and if she was in the truck at least I could reach her. Can you even put a cat tree in a truck you would have to take out the passenger seat. Where else could it fit?

"Miss Kitty, get down here. You better not hurt that squirrel and we are not bringing it on the truck so leave it alone." I sure hope she doesn't go any higher. "Get down here! That's it, back on down. Keep coming, all the way down here. Come on, you can do it." Why do cats think they have to chase things up a tree? Even the birds, when they know they can just fly away.

"Get back in the truck, we have a lot of cleaning to do. No more trees for now. I think I need to teach you how to sweep the floors since you are the one who makes the biggest messes."

Meow.

"Is that one of your balls out here on the ground? If you keep throwing them out, you aren't going to have any left in the truck to play with, I don't always see them. Hey, get back here, you need to pick it up and take it back in the truck with you." It's worse than having a kid, at least you can train a child how to pick up their own messes and not leave their toys outside.

I'm sure they have a laundromat at one of the truck stops on up the road, I'll try to stop early enough that we can get at least one load done. Why doesn't anyone invent a washer and dryer for the truck? Every driver would want one of them. They make them for campers, don't they? Maybe you could fit one in somewhere, I could put it up on the top bunk or something. How heavy are they? Would it break the bunk and fall on me while I was sleeping? Or maybe on the floor, across from the refrigerator on the other side. That would work, I would give up cupboard space for a washer and dryer. Would I have to have a water tank for it? How would the water drain after washing? No way I can get a truck into those RV dump things. How would that work? I guess that's why they don't have a washer or even a shower in a truck.

I think a movie will be the perfect end to the day. Maybe something funny. I'm not in the mood for those love stories, maybe Miss Kitty would like something with cats. Do they make funny cat movies? If not, I could probably take videos of some of the things Miss Kitty does and make a movie. She loves the phone pointed at her and seems to like it when I take pictures of her. I probably have more pictures of her than my kids. I need to call and check on everyone at home. Maybe I'll do that first, then a movie.

Everyone is fine and they all miss us. I can't just drop by to see them anytime I want. It takes a lot of planning to get loads that deliver close by so I can visit a while otherwise all I can do is get a load that allows me to go through there and maybe grab lunch or possibly get there late enough that I can spend one night before continuing with the load. I do what I can to get through there as often as possible.

I have a friend in Rochester New York, right on our route. Maybe I should give her a call, see if she is going to be around. She drives mostly local ever since she got hurt by all that stuff falling out and breaking the bones in her feet when she opened the doors on that trailer. There is a chance I can find the time to stop and say hi on the way through. She cooks homemade dinners and bakes deserts for me when I do get through there. I usually end up with a fridge full of leftovers. Maybe I should leave room in the refrigerator just in case. She might want to meet Miss Kitty.

I wonder if she still takes her dog 'Chief' on the truck with her? She has had him for a long time and he used to love running all over the country with her. I don't know if they allow pets when you do local deliveries. Does she have to drive a day cab? I think most local drivers do. I should ask her. That's another reason I don't want to drive local, I love having my bed so I can take a nap if I get tired. I also like having all my stuff in the truck with me. I think I better wait until I'm closer before I call, we might not have time and I don't want to get her hopes up if we can't stop.

"Are you ready to relax and watch a movie Miss Kitty? We can work on the leash another day but I think you need to watch a few of these videos of what a cat is supposed to do when they have a leash on. This won't be the last time we try the leash, we have just started your training."

Lord, thank you for a day of rest. Thank you for letting us find such a good place to park so we could get out of the truck for a while. Thank you for the good weather and the beauty all around. Thank you for all you have given us. Thank you again for Miss Kitty, what a blessing she is. Thank you, Lord.

Chapter 9

DID THEY SEE ME coming? All the other trucks went right on past. They just happen to turn the sign to open and gave me the red light as I got close to the weigh station? It figures, I have gotten a bypass on the scales all week, time to go through one so they can see all my paperwork is in order and permits up to date. You have to hit an open scale sooner or later. No worries, all my paperwork is up to date and I checked the truck out good this morning. I know my weight is good, I found a little mom and pop place that had a cat scale not far from the shipper. I didn't even have to slide the tandems on the trailer to adjust the weight.

I hope they don't mind that Miss Kitty is sitting on the dash, she is on her pillow. It's not like she's blocking the windshield, she just wants to see what's going on. I'm sure they see the same thing with those little dogs. I do have pet stickers on the doors so I'm not trying to hide her. She just likes to be seen. Maybe I need to give the truck a bath so they know how well I take care of my equipment, that always helps.

That's right, let me pass right on through and get back on the road. I think they have a quota on how many trucks they have to scale per month. I don't get called in for inspections very often but when I do it makes it worthwhile when I turn that clean inspection report in and get the $100 bonus on my check. I wonder if all the companies do that for their drivers?

Every state has a weigh station and most have multiple weigh stations throughout the state. The in-cab bypass is an invaluable tool to keep from having to stop at every open scale and using up a lot of extra drive time. Unfortunately, some companies have such a low rating due to multiple violations on their trucks they get called in every open scale so the bypass has no advantages to their drivers. I'm very fortunate to have a company with a good rating but I do still get called in on occasion. My clean inspections help keep a good rating for my company.

Time really has no meaning when you are out on the road. You make sure you pick up the load on time and deliver it on time but other than that, time is meaningless. Day of the week is nothing because you work 7 days a week. Other than what's required for getting your load taken care of, date and month mean nothing. Holidays don't really matter when you can't be home with your family so they are meaningless, it's just another work day. If you want time off you have to request it in time to plan the loads just right to get you to the place you need to be. They can't always get you to where you want to go but if dispatch is doing the planning right, they can usually get you close. It all depends on the loads.

Winter is the only time of the year you really have to pay attention to. Where to stop for the night because days are short, roads get slick and truck stops fill up fast. Make sure you keep plenty of fuel in the tanks, you don't want to run out, sometimes you have to keep the truck running to keep warm and everything from freezing. A lot more accidents happen and roads get shut down. Slower travel means lower miles which means lower pay so you have a lot of drivers who try to run too fast for the conditions. Keep extra food and water in the truck because you might get stuck somewhere that there's no food or water available. Make sure you can keep warm if the truck isn't running, you don't want to freeze to death. It does happen out here. These are things you need to think about when you live on the road. Extra supplies are a must.

You might haul the same product or a something different every time, that doesn't matter, all you really need to focus on is the weight and securement of the load. You need a load to haul if you want paid so it doesn't matter what it is as long as you have a load. You need to know the weight of the load if the conditions are bad so you don't get blown over or slide down a mountain out of control.

There are tons of rules and regulations you have to know and follow so this is not a job for a lazy person or one who doesn't care about rules. You are responsible for so many things from the time you pick up a load till the time you deliver it. The rules change a lot so you have to keep up with all the new things coming out. And you thought school was hard.

This is not a 9-5, or a 40-hour workweek job. You're only allowed to show 70 hours of on duty and driving combined per week and the driving is the only thing most drivers are paid for so most drivers go off duty as much as possible to have as many drive hours as possible and that usually means you work over 70 hour per week. Yes, you bend the rules to stay legal but you do it in order to make money. There is no overtime pay and unless you have to go to the hospital, there is no calling in sick. No one can cover for you for a day.

This is trucking, it's not easy and it's definitely not for everyone. It's a hard life and rather lonely most of the time. I'd like to say drivers stick together or you can all be friends but it's not like that. You do meet other drivers and you do build friendships but not everyone out here is friendly. Get used to being called names and being treated like trash because no one likes a truck driver. Shippers and receivers need you but they don't always like you. Most people even think your lazy or not all there in the head. They have no idea how hard you have to work, what you have to put up with or how many hours you put in every single day.

It gets lonely out here and so it makes life easier to have a pet with you. You don't feel so alone and they never judge you for who you are or what you do. It's not unusual to see a dog in a truck but not a lot of people have a cat on the truck. Some people are curious about a cat on a truck. Mostly how they handle going all over the country without running away. It might be a little difficult I suppose but at least you don't have to stop all the time for them to go potty and they don't care if you aren't paying attention to them all the time. They don't mind if you drive all day or all night. They like to sleep a lot. Although, Miss Kitty truly is special, it's as if she was made to be a truck cat. She likes to see the sights and smell the smells but she loves her truck. She might have been the best decision I ever made.

The radio is great for long runs but you lose stations all the time unless you pay for satellite radio. Audio books help the time pass faster but you have to make sure you can still focus on the road. If it's distracting, don't listen to them. I think I have listened to over 3,000 books over the years. A lot of drivers prefer talk radio but I like stories that take me to different places and have a lot of action. Everyone to their own.

Getting mail is very difficult so having a mail center in a town you go through frequently and can get a truck into, though you will most likely have to drop the trailer somewhere, is almost a must. I don't know how may jury summons I have received months after the trial date had already passed. You think they would quit sending them. I have to call them over and over notifying them that I am a truck driver and don't receive the request in time to do jury duty. I don't think they care. I think Miss Kitty actually got one before. She would have liked that; she would definitely vote guilty regardless of the evidence.

That's life on the road, love it or leave it. It's not for the weak and it's not for the lazy. If you can't handle being alone or by yourself a lot, I mean all the time, this might not be a good fit.

Lord, thank you for today, good or bad you are always with us, watching over us and protecting us. Thank you, Lord.

Chapter 10

IT'S FREEZING IN HERE. I better get the truck started, I need to warm up the engine so nothing freezes and leaves us broke down. Brrrr! I can hardly wait for the coffee to get done this morning. I should have turned the heat on last night. If I had known it was going to freeze, I would have left the truck running all night. I hope the truck warms up fast, it's cold.

"Are you warm enough Miss Kitty? I'm sorry I let it get so cold in here. No, we aren't getting out to do the pretrip yet, I have to have my coffee first this morning. It's too cold to get out there."

It shouldn't be this cold; it's not winter yet. No way I'm getting out on the road right now, it looks like it's a sheet of ice. Some drivers are foolish enough to drive on ice but I try to avoid it if at all possible. I don't want to end up in a ditch or a big pile up. No load is worth my life or anyone else's. Brrr, I think I might be a little jealous of Miss Kitty's fur coat.

"No, you don't get to have the window down right now, you can wait till it warms up a bit."

Meow.

"Don't argue with me, it's cold outside."

Meow.

"Alright, you have 5 seconds to sniff the air then the window goes back up."

Hiss.

"I told you so, the window stays up. Go play with a toy for a little while and let me drink my coffee and then maybe it will warm up a little before we go outside to do our pretrip."

Squeal, crunch.

"It's a good thing we didn't head out right away Miss Kitty, looks like that driver slid off the road on his way out. He looks stuck, we might have to wait for the tow truck to get him out of the way before we can leave."

Thank goodness the coffee is hot, I don't know if I could get up on such a cold day without it. I'd hate to be a tow truck driver in the winter. Winter hasn't even truly begun yet and he is already out here pulling trucks out of ditches. I wonder if he hates getting up in the wee hours to help all the cars and trucks in the snow and ice? Now that's not a job for just anyone, for sure. Bet he drinks a lot of coffee.

"What are you looking at? Do you like all the activity out there? Do you need up on the dash to see everything better Miss Kitty? Do you like watching the lights on the tow truck? Don't get up against the windshield, you might freeze to it."

"Looks like he is getting the truck out of the way, are you ready to get out and do our pretrip? Don't slip on the steps. Hey, where are you going? Ha ha, did your paws get frozen? Ok, you sit in the nice warm truck while I do the pretrip by myself today." She made it to the first step, sniffed and went back inside. I wonder if they make little booties for kitties? She might need them if she wants to get out on the ice in the mornings. What do the doggies do? They have to go out because they don't have a potty box to use. I feel sorry for all the dogs out here now.

I'll have to remember to check all my fluids when I stop for a break later on in the day since I already have the truck running and I'm not shutting it off just to check them now. Maybe Miss Kitty can get out and do a pretrip with me then. Hopefully it will be warmer. I might need to get her a little doggie jacket to help keep her warm. I'm not sure how she will feel about that. Do they make one for cats? They need to have a little more stretch to them than the ones for dogs.

I have a friend in San Antonio who is doing local driving now that she is starting her own business making crafts and stuff, maybe I'll give her a call and see how the weather is there. I know it's warmer than up here. I could get a load down to see her. There shouldn't be any problems getting a load to San Antonio and there are plenty of loads going out. If I can get there on a Friday or Saturday, I might stay the weekend and visit her for a day or possibly two. I can't take Miss Kitty to her house; she has big dogs and is allergic to cats. I think I'll wait just a bit, it might be better if we plan that trip after the snow hits, it almost never snows in San Antonio.

"Time to hit the road Miss Kitty, we need to go slow for a little while to see how slick the roads are. You need to stay in your seat." Maybe I should buy her some sort of a seatbelt, I think they have them for dogs. She would be really mad if I started getting her a bunch of stuff made for dogs. I guess she wouldn't know that everything was made for dogs. I'll tell her it's a kitty jacket and kitty boots and a kitty belt. Just in case she does understand. Just how smart are cats?

I hope it warms up soon, these roads are still pretty slick. So far, there have only been a few cars off the road but the trucks might be next. Too many drivers in a hurry this morning and we could have a disaster. Uh oh, nothing but brake lights ahead, looks like we are coming to a stop. Most likely an accident. Let's hope everyone is ok. Complete stop. That's never a good sign.

"What are you doing Miss Kitty? Are you flirting with that driver? Quit showing off, he doesn't want to watch you play. Now look what you've done, he has his phone out and is taking pictures of you. Are you trying to get famous? You never look that cute when no one is watching you. Do you stay up all night playing in the window for the drivers at the truck stops? You are shameless." I've seen her do that at night, she can't play innocent with me.

I have a feeling I'm going to find pictures or videos of her online one of these days. She loves attention but she doesn't want anyone getting too close to her. She loves it when people point their phones her direction but hates when people try to pet her. Little Miss Diva. Maybe I should post pictures and stories about her myself, maybe even a few videos. Hmm, that's something to think about.

"No, you don't need the window down. You can't sniff him from here anyway. I bet he has a dog in the truck with him. Sit back down, the traffic is starting to move again."

Oh my, that doesn't look good. A truck and a couple cars all smashed up. Looks like that car tried to fit under the trailer like on the 'Fast and the Furious'. When will they learn? Not saying the truck didn't slide into them but these types of accidents are usually caused by the impatient car drivers trying to get past the slow truck.

Lord, please let everyone be alright and protect the drivers out here today, the roads are nasty and the drivers are being stupid. Keep us safe and let us avoid hitting each other. Keep us on the road. Thank you, Lord.

"Sliding down the road, in a truck filled with food, oh what fun we'll have today, sliding all the way." Why am I trying to sing about this? I can't even carry a tune. Leave the song writing to someone who can sing or carry a tune or even make sense.

Thank goodness the roads are starting to clear up. Each hill had me worried; going up that I might slip and slide or coming down that this truck might turn into a sled. The ice is melting from the heat of everyone driving on them more than the temperature warming up. At least it is melting.

Thank you, Lord, for your protection out here on the roadways, especially in the worst of conditions, I know you are with us and protecting us. Thank you, Lord.

Chapter 11

"MISS KITTY, GET BACK here! What on earth are you chasing? Is that a rat? Leave it alone, you don't want to mess around with a rat. Get back here!"

Where is she going? Oh no, she better not run into those pallets after that rat. No! What is she thinking? It looks like those pallets are all broken and piled up like they are ready to have a bon fire. Where did she disappear to?

When we got here, they couldn't get us in a door right away so they said to park out back for a couple hours. Well, a couple hours to Miss Kitty means time to get out and play. I never would have let her out of the truck at a customer but there aren't any other trucks parked back here and there is plenty of room as well as plenty of time to let her get out for a little bit. I didn't think about there being rats back here. How was I supposed to know? Now what am I supposed to do? I can't climb into that pile of pallets; they might break and I'd probably get stuck in there. It looks like there might be a whole family of rats in there.

"Miss Kitty! Get out of there! Leave the rat alone, he might bite you." Do rats carry disease? I think I read somewhere they do, didn't I? I can't remember.

"What's all the commotion out here? Ma'am we are ready for you now, I was just coming to get you."

Wonderful, they are finally ready for us and Miss Kitty is playing with a rat.

"I'm sorry, my cat saw a rat and chased it into that pile of pallets, I'm trying to get her to come out."

"Oh my, I'll see if I can't get someone out here with a forklift, we don't want her getting hurt in there or left here."

"Thank you. I'm sorry about this, I wouldn't have let her out but she usually stays right around the truck and we had such a long time to wait. I didn't even think about her getting into those pallets." I hate that they have to rescue my cat but I'm not climbing in there. He seemed understanding about the situation, not mad or anything. I sure hope we don't get in trouble for this.

Meow, meow, merow, owr, meow.

"Are you stuck? Please tell me you aren't stuck Miss Kitty. You need to get out of there. You do not want to stay up here in New York for the winter. It's too cold."

She better come out of there. Lord, please get her out.

"EEK! Here comes your rat Miss Kitty! Get it! Do you see it? Come get it Miss Kitty. Hah, Gotcha! You let the rat go back home, you've had enough fun for today and we might be in trouble. They were going to have to get a forklift out here to move all those pallets to get to you and they might have fallen on you. You are lucky you didn't get hurt in there."

"Here comes the guy now. Hurry up and get in the truck."

"I see you're back in the truck, were you able to get your cat out Ma'am? We don't have a forklift available right now to move the pallets."

"Yes, thank you. She is back in the truck. Do you want me to get in a door now?"

"Please, if you would, we should have you unloaded in no time. Thanks for waiting. Go ahead and go to door 12."

I wish all the shippers and receivers were as nice as they are here. Wouldn't that be great. I am so very grateful we didn't get in trouble for Miss Kitty being out of the truck. I really am going to have to be more careful about that. We really do need to work on that leash.

"Yuck, are those fleas all over you? Oh my goodness, you need a bath! They are going to be all over the truck. How am I going to get rid of them?"

There better be a store close by that has flea stuff. What can I use on the truck? We can't use any kind of poison. How do you get rid of fleas?

They are going to be everywhere. Maybe Wal-Mart has something, google says there is a Wal-Mart not too far from here. I'm heading there as soon as we are empty. They might have to wait a while before I can get the next load, this is an emergency.

I see a collar and a bunch of shampoo stuff but I can't use that in the truck. How do I get them out of the truck? Out of her bed? Out of my bed? I need to get a few of those collars, just in case this ever happens again. All the natural stuff seems to be made with peppermint oil, that won't hurt Miss Kitty, will it? This spray looks good, it says it's safe around children and pets. I can cut up one of the flea collars and put little pieces around the bed and wherever she might lay. This better work. I'm going to have to do laundry. Am I going to have to do laundry every day? I hope this next load has extra time on it, I'm going to be doing a lot of cleaning or our truck will become the next flea nest.

Dear Lord, I know I ask a lot of you on a daily basis and you watch over me every day out here on the road but I come to you today asking for you to kill or at least remove the critters who have moved into my truck. If you want them to live, can you please tell them to find another home? I do not want them in mine. I don't care how you do it but please get rid of them. Thank you so much, Lord.

This truck is only big enough for two of us, there is absolutely no room for thousands of little critters running around trying to eat us. Man is this stuff strong smelling; it better be working. Choke… Maybe too strong. This brush sure seems to be getting a lot of them off Miss Kitty. Thank goodness. Good thing I bought that little hand vac, it makes cleaning them off the bed so much easier. I hope that by cutting up that flea collar and putting some of the pieces in the vacuum it kills them so they don't get back out and multiply even more.

What a nightmare. I can feel little bugs crawling all over me even if they aren't really there. Just knowing they are in the truck is almost more than I can deal with. How do I know when they are all gone or that they won't come back? Do I just keep using this stuff for a few days or weeks and then stop? What is the lifespan of a flea? How long does it take to hatch the babies? Do you ever completely get rid of them? Do they hibernate?

This has been quite the day. I never want to go through this again. I'm going to be cleaning for a long time trying to get rid of these things. I'm debating on whether to even let Miss Kitty out of the truck again. She doesn't have to go outside for anything, I know she likes to explore but this is a bit overwhelming and I really don't want to do this again. Do dogs go through this? They have to go outside all the time. How do drivers handle it when the dogs bring home little critters?

Dear Lord, please remove the creepy crawly critters and guard the truck from any coming back. Don't let any hide or lay eggs in the truck. Thank you for there being a store close by to get the stuff needed to get them off the truck. Keep them off Miss Kitty please. Thank you, Lord.

Chapter 12

FLORIDA FOR THE WEEKEND. Do people really dream about this? Do they know about the unbelievable amount of traffic and the tourists who slam on their brakes all of a sudden because they think they might have missed their turn? The families who are trying to find Disney world in Orlando and as soon as they see it from the interstate, they think they have to slow down or they might miss it. Not slow to take an exit but slow to like twenty miles an hour so they can look at it as they drive by. Daytona, where the traffic for the races has the interstate blocked for miles while everyone tries to get off at the exit at the same time. Miami, where you had best keep your doors locked and windows up and by all that is holy, don't stop unless it's an emergency. I don't think there is any time of the year that is not tourist season.

To top it off, this is a holiday weekend. Halloween, nothing like everyone dressed in crazy costumes doing crazy things at all hours of the night. The whole weekend is one big party or something. I really need to focus on the positive. It is beautiful, the palm trees are a nice change of scenery. Is that an alligator in the road? Just stay positive. Ok, I just dropped in Winter Haven which is a pretty cute town just a little West of Orlando. There are a few little areas you can pull off to see the lakes or ponds in some cases. That's pretty. It's hot, so much better than the icy weather we had up North. Green. Who am I kidding? It's humid and I don't want to stay too long down here. In and out. That's the way to enjoy Florida. I don't hate it, I just don't want to stay too long.

I'm in San Antonio, Florida, that's so funny to me. Or maybe this is Dade City here at the Flying J. Whichever. I have to have the trailer washed out before picking up the next load which won't be ready until Monday morning at three. They have a blue beacon here so I can get the trailer washed out, park for the weekend, go inside to shower and grab a bite to eat. I might even get to do my laundry if the machines aren't all full. Thrilling. Boy, this place gets packed fast. I'm glad I got here while there's still parking available.

"Halloween is not a night for kitties to be out. You better stay in the truck and be good. Bad things happen to little kitties on Halloween."

Meow.

"We can watch Halloween movies and I'll give you extra treats just like trick or treating. Does that sound good to you? Let's watch some funny movies so you won't have nightmares tonight."

Meow.

"I could have bought you that costume at the store. Do you want to wear a doggie costume for Halloween? They didn't have anything cute for kitties. Bet a lot of drivers would look at you then. That doggie parked next to us at the fuel island earlier had on a cute costume."

Meow.

"Some people give doggies a treat especially when they have a costume on. Of course, they would probably just give you a doggie treat because I don't think there are any of them who have treats for kitties. No one thinks about kitties in the trucks."

Meow.

"I agree, how rude. You work just as hard as the doggies out here. They should keep special treats for you too."

"Remember that little gray kitty we saw yesterday? He looked like he enjoyed riding in a truck. I think once drivers start seeing more kitties out here, they will all want a kitty too. Everyone needs a kitty."

Meow.

"I didn't decorate the truck for Halloween, maybe we should start doing that. I usually only decorate for Christmas. Do you think we need to start decorating the truck for every holiday? You won't tear everything down if I do, will you? Do you like decorations? We might try Thanksgiving but

Christmas is a must. I kind of wish we had thought about all the decorating stuff before Halloween, we could have done some pretty cool things to the truck."

Meow.

I wonder what the kids are doing for Halloween. Mine are all grown up and have kids of their own now. They barely know who their grandma is. She comes to town a couple times a year spends a couple days buying stuff and taking everyone out to eat then is gone again. I wish I could get through there more often but it's hard to find freight in and out of there. I bet they are all trick or treating tonight. The kids will probably send pictures of everyone in their costumes. I hope they get lots of candy.

It's a shame that I have to interact with my family mostly through Facebook. That's how I find out what the kids are up to, see pictures as they grow and the school stuff like what grades they are in. Maybe I can get through soon. It's so hard. I don't even realize how much time has gone by till I get to town and see how big the kids have grown since the last time I saw them. I do feel a little guilty for not being there more. I miss them so very much but if I didn't work, I couldn't send them extra money every now and then or do so much with them when I do get to town.

You make a lot of sacrifices as a driver. You have to work through almost all the holidays and miss birthdays, special events and special occasions. You try to get home as much as possible but the loads don't always cooperate.

Let's see what's on tv, I bet they have a lot of movies for Halloween with kitty cats. I might not have my kids but I have Miss Kitty so I'm not alone this year. She might not like watching tv much but she lays on me and snuggles while I watch. That means a lot. She is family too.

"Come on Miss Kitty, we have time to watch a movie before bedtime. Stay away from the windows tonight, please."

Thank you, Lord, for watching over us and protecting us from all the crazies out there celebrating tonight. Keep us safe. Thank you, Lord.

Chapter 13

JUST WONDERFUL, WE HAVE a wheel seal leaking. It sure was a good thing we stopped here at the TA to fuel, they have a shop right here. Let me go see how long before they can get us in. It shouldn't take too long to fix; I can grab something for lunch while they are working on it so we won't have to stop again down the road. It's a good thing I spotted that now, no way I want to lose a wheel or have it catch fire. It's always a good idea to check the tires when you stop, just in case something like this happens.

Good deal, we are getting right in. Thank you, Lord.

"Be good for the mechanic while I'm inside, he's just going to get the truck fixed up so it doesn't break down out on the road."

"That sure is a pretty cat you have. I have a few cats at home but I don't think any of mine would like riding in a truck so much. She seems to like being in the truck. Go on in and get you a bite to eat, we will be fine out here."

"You might not want to reach into the truck, she is a little protective of her truck. If you need in there for any reason, let her sniff you first and if she acts even a little aggressive just have them call me and I'll come right back out here."

"Don't you worry, I get along great with animals. Want to smell me? Here, you can sniff my hand. See, I'm a good guy. Awe, you want scratches? Like those ears rubbed? Do you want that belly rubbed? You're such a good kitty, yes you are." He really has a way with cats or at least this cat.

"Wha… what the heck? Miss Kitty, do you like him? You are letting him pet you? Really? Wow, you really do have a way with cats. I have never seen her so friendly with a stranger before."

"Don't worry, she is in good hands, go on in and get you a bite to eat, we'll be just fine." He seems confident. I hope Miss Kitty behaves herself.

"Thanks."

I was starting to wonder if she liked anyone, good to know she can be friendly when she wants to. Maybe I can go on in without worrying about what she might do.

***

Ring, ring.

"Your truck is done. You can come sign the bills and you're good to go."

"Thanks, I'll be right there."

That didn't take too long, just enough time to eat. Good deal.

Why is everyone gathered around the truck? Did Miss Kitty bite someone? Did they find another problem with the truck? I better get over there and find out.

"What is going on here? Is there something wrong with the truck? They said it was all done."

"Nah, we just want to pet the kitty." The mechanics all seem to love her.

"She is letting people pet her?"

"Everyone except the gals from the office. I think she likes the grease smell and they don't have it. She won't let anyone touch her that doesn't smell like grease. It's hilarious. All the guys out here want to see if she will let them pet her."

"She hasn't tried to bite anyone?" I am literally shocked.

"Only tried to get one of us, Jim just came in to work smelling all fresh and clean and she wouldn't let him get close to her but just before you came back out, he walked back up to her and she was fine with him. He's doing an oil change on that truck over there and when he walked over to her, he must have smelled like oil or something because she let him pet her then. That's how we knew it was the grease and oil smell that she likes. We have all been coming over to her to see how she reacts. I hope you don't mind."

"That's great to know, I'm glad you guys figured it out for me. Ha ha ha. I will have to keep a greasy rag by my seat so when someone asks to pet her, I'll give them the rag and tell them they have to get their hands greasy first. I bet not that many people would want to try and pet her then. That's too funny." Wait till I tell Babygirl about this. The kids would love to get greasy I'm sure but the adults might be a different story. They will love to hear about Miss Kitty and the mechanics. They love to hear stories about what she does out here on the road.

"Is that why you like doing pretrips with me in the mornings, Miss Kitty? Do you like the smell of the oil and grease? Is that why you love being on the truck? Just don't come back in covered in grease. Keep the grease outside of the truck, ok?"

That's something I might have to watch out for, if she jumps in here covered in grease it will be really hard to get it cleaned up and she would probably spread it everywhere as much as she jumps around. Yuck. Does that mean she likes the taste of it too? Cats clean themselves by licking so if she is all covered in grease, she would be licking grease. Double yuck. Do dogs like grease? I don't see them sniffing greasy stuff or getting all greasy.

It's a little out of the way but I think I can swing through to see the family on the way to Washington. Just watch, everyone is going to be more excited to see Miss Kitty than they will me. They're all so curious how she is doing and if she likes being on the truck. I send them pictures of her and tell them some of the cute things she does. In a way, she is famous, to the family at least. The star returns home for a visit to tell of all her adventures. I wonder what stories she would tell if we could understand her?

I'll make sure we get there in time to have dinner and visit with everyone. If I can plan it just right, we can stay the night there. It will take a little extra time, going local highways instead of the interstates but the miles should be about the same. It's all in how I do the trip planning. I better get the fuel routing figured out, there aren't a whole lot of acceptable fuel stops though there. It's a good thing I know where they are. Most companies keep their trucks away from the Western slope of Colorado. Usually, the trucks bring in loads to Denver and then local companies get the loads over to the Western slope for all the stores. There is no way in or out of there without traveling a mountain pass and some drivers don't do well in the mountains. I was born and raised there so I have no problems with mountain driving. I do try to avoid winters there, which is why I don't see the family as much as I would like to.

Winters didn't used to bother me so much. Chaining up didn't bother me that much either. Is it because of how much older I am getting or is it that I've done it for so long I just don't want to do it anymore? I've spent years out here and chained up more times than I can possibly count but unless I absolutely have to, I don't want to. It doesn't matter what anyone else thinks, I'm the one driving the truck, they can worry about their own problems and keep their judgements to themselves, thank you very much.

I wonder if I can get on one of those Southern routes for the winter? That sounds nice. I don't want to be stuck on it during the summer months, it would be too hot then. Who wants to be hot during the summer? I just want to give the new guys a chance to get experience driving in the snow through the winter, that's all. I really like going North in the summer. Have you seen Washington or Montana in the summer? It's absolutely gorgeous. Sometimes I feel like I'm driving through a painting. The colors are so rich and even the mountains have different colors. The dirt itself has different colors and then the trees in the sun have different shades of green and in the shade, they are different shades of blues.

I've tried to tell people how beautiful it is driving all over the country and seeing the things you have only read about. It's hard for me to describe that to people. Everyone experiences things in a different way. I like watching the sun rise and fill everything with light in the mornings like its breathing life into everything. It feels light as well as bright. I also love the colors of the sunsets where everything takes on richer, heavier colors. It's as if the colors have a different weight as the sun goes down.

I've tried to explain the difference in the colors of green in different states or how somethings look blue at one angle and green at a different angle when you drive by. I've tried to describe how the ocean looks different than a lake. How mountains are different in the North than they are in the South. Things look different in the East than they do in the West. I tell people they need to experience those things; you can't feel it from a picture. I wish I could explain it to them but they could never see things the way I do and I can't see them the way they do. Some things can only be experienced by the individual seeing it.

Ask a driver why they like driving and you will get a different answer from each one. The freedom of not having a boss looking over your shoulder all the time, the open road with endless possibilities, the scenery or whatever it is that has beauty, it's something that goes soul deep. It takes something special to do this type of work and make the sacrifices. And to be alone so much of the time. Do everything by yourself. Go everywhere by yourself. It's like being a gypsy or a nomad, you might say.

Ugh, traffic is picking up, people must be getting off work, I should start looking for a place to shut down for the night. That's the reason I get up so early, so I can shut down before the traffic gets too bad and the truck stops fill up. It can be very difficult finding a place to park. I try to keep my driving to a little over 600 miles a day so I don't get so burned out on driving. It also keeps me from running out of hours in the wrong places, if I plan my trips right.

Thank you, Lord, for all the wonders you have given us to enjoy and for watching over us and keeping us safe out here. You paint such beauty all around us. You are with us each day in all we do. Thank you, Lord.

Chapter 14

I WAS RIGHT, EVERYONE was so excited to see Miss Kitty. Everyone was waiting for us when we pulled in. I didn't even get the truck parked before they all started coming towards the truck to see her.

"Miss Kitty, how did you like driving all over the country?"

"Miss Kitty, how do you like living in a big truck?"

"Miss Kitty, did you have fun out on the road?"

"Miss Kitty, are you glad to be home?"

"Miss Kitty, are you excited to go back out on the road again?"

"Miss Kitty, did you meet any new friends?"

"Miss Kitty, are you going to stay and visit for a while?"

"Miss Kitty, did you miss us?"

"Hello to you guys too, Miss Kitty says hi and yes and no to all your questions."

"Sorry, hi mom, we've missed you." Said Babygirl.

"Yea, we love you too mom." Said my son.

"Can we take Miss Kitty to the restaurant with us?"

"Can Miss Kitty sleep with me tonight?"

"Can I hold Miss Kitty?"

"Sorry, they won't let Miss Kitty into the restaurant and she doesn't like people food. We can't stay, we are only here one night. We have to leave early in the morning before you get up so she has to sleep on the truck. She has missed you guys and loves you."

"Did you like having her on the truck with you?" Said Babygirl in a bit of a worried tone.

"It has been very interesting to have a cat on the truck with me and yes, she has had fun. She has missed everyone and you guys can take turns climbing up into the truck to visit her but don't crowd her all at once."

The questions are coming so fast I can't even keep track of who is asking what, I hope this doesn't freak Miss Kitty out. I don't know how she feels about crowds like this. Did I answer everyone's questions? I don't normally get this kind of a greeting. Usually, one of the kids comes to get me and I go visit them for a while then we go up to the other one's house and visit there for a while then we go shopping and after that, one of them brings me back to the truck.

Even my mom and sibling showed up to greet Miss Kitty. This really is a special occasion. Not that we don't see each other but it is extremely unusual for everyone to come all together to see me as soon as I get to town. This calls for something really special.

"Alright guys, who wants to go to Olive Garden?" Everyone loves Olive Garden; everyone should be happy with that decision. How many cars are we going to have to take? I don't want to leave Miss Kitty alone for too long, we can come straight back and grab her then go visit with everyone. I hope she doesn't get too overwhelmed by all the attention, especially with the younger kids.

***

Dinner is very expensive with so many people. That's ok, this doesn't happen very often so it's nice to be able to do this for everyone. My little gift. It feels so wonderful to do such small simple things and make such a good memory with the family.

"Miss Kitty, would you like to visit everyone now? I'm sorry we couldn't take you with us but you wouldn't have liked the restaurant anyhow. Are you ready to see the kids? No biting, please."

Meow.

***

Whew! What a night, everyone wanted to hold Miss Kitty, talk to her and pet her until she finally climbed into her carrier to hide from everyone. I could tell she was ready to leave. They all loved her so much and other than a few growls and hisses at the kids, she seemed to be just fine with all the attention and at least some of the loving.

No one wanted us to leave but they all understood, it's been this way for many years now. They all told Miss Kitty bye and wished her safe travels. I think I heard a few whispered comments to her about how she needed to take care of me too. That was sweet. It was so wonderful to visit with everyone.

"Miss Kitty, did you like all that? Thank you for putting up with everyone without biting anyone. It shouldn't be quite so bad the next time we come to town. You handled it all very well and I am very proud of you. What do you say we try to get some sleep before it's time get up and head out."

Meow.

She might actually be more exhausted than me tonight. We still have a very long trip ahead of us, we are just a little over half way there. This is the best time of the year to see Colorado, all the leaves are changing color and it's so beautiful. From the time we first entered the state, that's the first thing we noticed. Coming this route lets us go through the most scenic parts of the state. Utah will have a little color but they can't compete with Colorado.

Lord, thank you for giving us all the beauty of this trip. Thank you for giving us the time to stop and see everyone. Thank you for giving me the finances to buy and enjoy a good meal with the family all together. Thank you for allowing the time to visit and catch up with the lives of all the family. Thank you for all you do for us, Lord.

Chapter 15

~~

I'M SO THANKFUL WE didn't have to go into Seattle. I prefer to stay on the outskirts. I don't think it would impress Miss Kitty to see the space needle. There really isn't much to see from the ground but from what I hear, you can go up into it and it's absolutely spectacular. I wouldn't know, I just get to drive by on the way to the docks to pick up or deliver. Maybe someday I'll be able to get out of the truck to see the country as regular folks see it. I only get to see things from a distance, just see the little I can glimpse as I pass by. People travel thousands of miles to see things and are able to get out and enjoy all the sights. Sometimes I envy them a little.

Miss Kitty loves the smell of everything up here. She wants her window to be down all the time. I think she gets offended when I close it to drive. There is no way I will take the chance of her falling out when the truck is moving. She knows that but she still wanted it open at every red light or stop sign. She knows she has to wait until we get parked at the receiver. I don't smell anything great here.

We were able to get right in and deliver the load. Dispatch had another load lined up before we were unloaded so we can head out right away. I love it when things work like that and we don't have to wait around for a load.

Looks like they are scarce on loads coming out of Washington again. Double pickup, Brewster then Yakima. Good deal, I'll be heading to Cleburne Texas, I should be able to grab my mail from Texarkana since it's fairly close. At least closer than I have been in a few months. I better check If they have a load going that direction so I won't have to deadhead all the way over there. I could have tried to get it on the way from Florida but that would have put me a little too far out of route to go through Colorado and see the family.

I really do like coming up here to Brewster, they have a grocery store across the street from the shipper that cooks ribs. They might not be as good as the ones in Texas but man do I love ribs. Prices are bit high up here so I try not to get a whole lot of groceries but I like grabbing a few things. Sometimes I can shop while they load the truck. Better check in so I know if I have time to run over to the store.

"Hi, I'm here to pick up a partial load for Wal-Mart in Cleburne."

"*I'm sorry, we are still waiting on the product. We probably won't have it till tomorrow.*" They informed me nicely. I'm sure they have to deal with a lot of angry drivers when they tell them this kind of news.

"What do you mean you won't have the product till tomorrow? I'm only getting a partial load here and I'm supposed to pick up the second part of this load this afternoon in Yakima." No, please don't do this.

"*There is nothing we can do right now; we don't have the product to ship. You'll have to wait.*"

Dispatch is going to love this. They will have to let the customer in Yakima know, I don't even know for sure when they'll get the product here let alone when I can be there to get that part of the load. Time to give them the wonderful news. I better call them now to let them know.

"*Don't tell me, they don't have the product.*"

"It sounds like I didn't need to call, you already knew."

"*We've had two other drivers try to get loads out of there already and they told them they didn't have the product.*"

"Then why did you dispatch me on the load?"

"*Because the customer wants the product and it's our job to get it and take it to them.*"

"I know that but if they don't have product why are you sending trucks up here."

"*You said they will have the product tomorrow, right?*" Dispatch sounds so hopeful.

"Yes."

"*You might be the first truck we have sent up there this week that actually gets loaded. We are trying to keep our end of the contract with Wal-Mart. All the companies are having problems getting product from there and we have been shipping partial loads from Yakima all week. Wal-Mart is getting really upset, let's see if we can help fix that by actually getting a full load for them.*"

"I'll try, I'm not the one who is short on product and I can't pick up what's not here."

"*Just do the best you can.*"

"Gee, thanks."

Click.

I don't think Yakima is too worried about how fast I get there, they aren't picking up the slack or lack and are only sending the partial load that was ordered from there. By the sound of things, it's getting worse up here. This happens every now and then but it's usually not this bad. If I am able to get a full load, Wal-Mart is going to love me. I mean, if they cared about me, they would. Well, this leaves me with plenty of time to go shopping. I am definitely having those ribs tonight.

"Well, Miss Kitty, what should we do today? It's not even noon and we have to wait until who knows when tomorrow."

Meow.

"You want to try the leash again?"

Meowow.

"You are going to have to get used to it. It's required by law in some places."

Meow.

"Come on, let's get the harness on. Yes, that's part of it. Stand still, I need to get this latched. Miss Kitty, you are going to have to cooperate."

Meowowl, meow.

"Stand up, it does not paralyze you to wear it. Someone might see you flopped here. Do you want them to take a picture of you like this? Stand up and take a few steps. It won't hurt, I promise. I'll give you a treat if you walk."

Flop.

"Three steps, really? You can do more than that. It didn't hurt to walk those three steps; it won't hurt to walk more. I don't feel sorry for you. You're making a fool of yourself, get up and walk like a normal cat. Yes, normal cats walk on leashes."

Meow.

"Miss Kitty, we have been out here for almost an hour and you haven't even taken 10 steps. You are not hurt, you're not dead, get up. Fine, I give up. You will have to do this sooner or later. I'm going to go to the store and grab my ribs. No, I'm not bringing you back anything from the store, you didn't earn a treat today. You need to do better if you want to earn a treat."

Meow.

"Nope, you have to do something to earn your treats, you don't just get them for doing nothing."

We did make a little progress today. Ten steps are a lot better than the first time we tried. This might take longer than I thought. How long is it supposed to take? How often are you supposed to work with a cat? I can't do it every day. I know they don't have this problem with dogs. They seem to like the leash. They might fight a little in the beginning but then they are completely fine with it. I haven't really given her a chance to get used to it yet. I'm sure it doesn't happen overnight for any cat. I probably need to learn a technique from someone who has done it before. I'm not going to give her treats all the time or she will get fat and lazy and might not ever want to learn. Will she do just enough for a treat and that's it? Or do they do what you want them to do after you withhold a treat just so you do give it to them when they do what you want? That might not be too bad then. If she would just take a few more steps, she would see how easy it is.

Yum, I got to the store at just the right time, these ribs are tender and juicy. Hits the spot. They might be a little pricey but they sure do taste good today. Too bad Miss Kitty doesn't like ribs. The only other thing close is McDonald's and I don't care for them much. Miss Kitty doesn't either. She doesn't really like people food at all as far as I know. I do have food on the truck but who passes up ribs?

***

Good, I'm the first driver here this morning. I wanted to make sure to get here before they opened so I would be first in line to get loaded just in case any product did come in. I don't want to spend another day up here waiting on the load. Here come a couple of drivers. I'm first guys. I just smile.

"Morning, looks like we are all waiting for them to open. Are you guys picking up or delivering?"

"*Picking up, I was supposed to pick up two days ago but they cancelled the load. I did a short run and they sent me back up here to get the load again.*" Said the first driver.

"*I'm delivering, had to wait all day yesterday to get loaded so I couldn't make it in time last night before they closed.*" Said the second driver.

"Step up here in front of me, you might have the product I've been waiting for." If he does, I can get loaded first thing this morning and have time to grab the load in Yakima and keep rolling today.

"*I don't want to cut in front of anyone.*"

"***Please do!***" Both the first driver and I said at the same time.

Finally, they are opening the doors. I step back to let the guy with the load in first, he has the product, he needs to be first to go in so they'll know whether they can load the rest of us.

"*Go ahead and get in door 3, as soon as we get the product off his truck, we will put it on yours and you can go pick up the rest of your load.*" Yes! That's what I wanted to hear.

"Thanks."

Thank you, Lord. Thank you for waking me up this morning. It was a good thing I was here the minute they opened the doors. I don't think all the other drivers out there waiting are going to be getting their loads for a while yet. Thank you, Lord.

Yakima didn't have any delays on product, we are on our way. Texas, we come! Only 2,000 miles to go.

Chapter 16

I WOULD STOP BACK by to see the family but I really need to get there as quickly as possible. Interstate almost all the way this time. I wish it was all interstate. Where's that fairy dust when you need it. Maybe they could install jet boosters on here to get this thing going a little faster. I'm not in a big hurry but I am running a day behind now. I don't know if I can make up for the time I lost waiting on the product.

Thank goodness Cabbage is dry. I don't want to mess with chains. It slows you down enough when it's dry, stopping to chain and then taking the chains off on the other side takes quite a bit of time and I don't have that kind of time to spare.

What's going on here? Construction? An accident? Come on people, let's get a move on. There is always a problem with traffic in Ontario. Maybe someone was in too big of a hurry and now we all have to wait. It's not like I'm going to make it there by the original appointment time they set anyhow. They won't accept the load if you are more than thirty minutes late. No use being in that much of a hurry, I want to make it there in one piece.

I'll have to stop in Ogden. I don't have the hours to make it to Evanston tonight. I think it's faster to run across I-80 then drop down to Denver and take the 287. I could possibly run down to Moab and take the 191 to I-40 and across to Amarillo then take the 287. Better not, stick to as much interstate as possible. Time is of the essence. I'm not in a race but I don't want to waste any time for sure. Play it safe out here. Just be quick about it.

***

The speed limit is 80 mph across Wyoming, they need to turn my truck up, I could probably make the appointment time if I could run 80 mph across. They tell me they can't because the steer tires are only rated to 75 mph, I say they need to get better steer tires. Most of Texas is like 80 or 85 mph too. Do you know how long it takes to drive across Texas? I think they should allow trucks to at least go the speed limit. Then again, some of those drivers can't keep it on the road at 65 mph. They might have a point. My truck does 73. Who sets a speed at 73? That just seems a bit ridiculous to me.

This has to be the worst stretch of the whole trip. There is nothing to look at, not many places to stop and it takes forever to get through Wyoming. I know why they set the speed limit up to 80 mph, all the drivers would fall asleep if they had to go too slow. Give me a tree every now and then or something to look at. Not even an audio books does that much good out here.

I might have to stop in Limon for the night. There are a few parking areas past that but I need to stop there to get fuel and I can't make it all the way to Lamar. Better just plan on that or maybe Hugo? Let's see how long it takes to get through the Denver area and go from there.

***

Made it to Hugo but I don't think I can do this last stretch in one day. If highway 287 was an interstate maybe. Do you know how many little towns are on highway 287? Better let dispatch know I need them to get the appointment moved back a day. I tried. It was too much to hope for with all the mountains and those little towns. Even on flat land it would have been pushing it and I'm not positive I would have been able to do it.

The hours of service keep you from driving too much and overdoing it. It also makes it to where the company you work for can't force you to run when you are too tired. They used to tell drivers they would fire them if they didn't keep going. Now, you get a total of 11 hours of drive time a day and then you have to shut down for 10 hours and take a rest break.

You can split it up a little if you need to take a nap for a couple hours but that's the guidelines and the way to split your hours with longer breaks can mess up your hours and your arrival times if you don't know what you are doing. You still can't violate the daily hours or the 70 hours driving and on duty per week limit.

***

So close! Just made it to the Loves in Rhome before I ran out of hours. Less than 60 miles to go. That was one heck of a trip. They rescheduled the appointment for four in the afternoon tomorrow. I wouldn't have tried to rush so much getting down here if I had known when they would get the load rescheduled for delivery a little bit earlier in the trip.

They have a dirt lot right next to Wal-Mart that trucks can park, I'll go ahead and leave out early and park there so I know I won't have any problems getting there. I'll park in the lot until an hour before the appointment time, that's as early as they allow you to check in.

***

"We made it Miss Kitty. I'll park over here at the back corner so you can get out for a bit. Don't run off and stay away from any fleas nests you might find. I'm going to fix a bite to eat while you play."

I might watch a movie or see what's on tv. I could take a little nap I suppose. Not while Miss Kitty is outside though. I'll let her play till I'm done eating.

***

"Finally, Miss Kitty, time to check in."

Meow.

Thankfully they have a door for us right away. I'll bet they have been waiting on this load for some time.

That was fast, got us unloaded and we are off to get the next load. Thank goodness this load is over. Thankfully dispatch was able to get us another load right away. We have had too much waiting on this load, we need to get some miles for our next check.

Lord, please let the next load be easier. Don't let there be problems or delays. Thank you, Lord.

Chapter 17

"Miss Kitty! Miss Kitty, come back. Miss Kitty. Please don't do this. Miss Kitty."

This load picked up at 7:30 pm. Things were going great, got the other load off, picked this load up, all I had to do was stop here and scale the load. I'm sitting here at the TA in Dallas. I don't know what to tell dispatch. I don't know what to do. I pulled onto the scale to get this load weighed so we could get out of Dallas asap. The app wouldn't work for scaling the load and I couldn't reach the button for them to do the scale from inside, so I opened the door to hit the button. Miss Kitty decided to jump out at that moment.

She gets in and out of the truck all the time so it shouldn't have been a big deal. I gave them the information to get the scale ticket and she still wasn't in the truck so I pulled off the scale and circled back around to the fuel island to park for a bit longer. I tried and tried to find her to get her back in the truck. She ran off into the bushes at the side of the scale. There isn't a whole lot of places in there for her to go. It's just a little strip between the truck stop and the road.

I called and called her, walked back and forth trying to see her. There's at a bit of a slope and I think there might be a ditch down there. I tried to go in as far as I could but the weeds are so tangled, I couldn't hardly move. The trucks were starting to really line up at the fuel pumps and a guy came out to tell me I had to move my truck. I moved it up the hill in the parking lot and parked it. You have 2 hours then it costs money to park. I thought I would be gone by then.

I walked back down the hill and searched again. I called out and walked back and forth but I couldn't find her. I have searched and searched. I stayed here all night trying to find her. I don't know where she is and dispatch has been calling me to find out why I'm still in Dallas. How can I leave? They have promised to try and find another driver to swap with me down the road so I can come back but chances of that are pretty slim. How do I leave her? I don't get through Dallas that often, who knows when I could actually get back. It's almost Thanksgiving and the loads are all in a rush to get to the stores in time, I could get stuck out East. I can't leave. Don't they understand that? They continue to call; I continue to search.

Lord, I am still here. I can't leave. Please Lord, where is Miss Kitty? Can't you bring her back to me? Is this it? Did I do something wrong? Why would she leave me? Please Lord, bring her back to me.

Ring, ring.

"No. I can't leave."

"*Tory, be reasonable. If she was going to come back, she would have already. Who knows where she went, Dallas is a very big place. We have got to get that load moving.*"

"I just can't leave her behind. I can't do it." Why can't they understand?

"*I know you care about her but she is just a cat, this load has to get delivered asap, they are waiting on it. Think of all the kids waiting for Thanksgiving dinner and they don't have their food because you can't find your cat.*"

"She isn't just a cat; she is my family. How do you think my Thanksgiving is going to be without her?"

"*You have an entire truck of turkeys; they have to get delivered asap.*"

"Who cares about turkeys, they can have a Thanksgiving ham. My cat is missing."

"*You have searched all night, if she wanted to be found she would have been found already. You have to get rolling. I promise, I'll get you back there as soon as possible but you have to get this load down the road.*" Pleads dispatch.

"You are heartless."

"*I'll buy you another cat, just get this load rolling. This is the last time I'm going to ask you.*"

"You can't replace a cat just like that. She is family. She is my family."

"Tory, I'm done talking. Get the load rolling." Dispatch issues the final warning.

Click.

Dear Lord God, please, I beg of you, send her to me. I have to leave here but I don't want to leave without her. I can't wait any longer, you know how many families depend on the food I bring. I have to do my job, I have to make my deliveries. Please, Lord.

"Miss Kitty! Please Miss Kitty, come back. Please, I don't want to leave you behind. Miss Kitty?"

What am I going to do? Do you know all the bad things that could happen to her? Where is she? Why? Why did she jump out and not come back? Where could she have gone to? I can't do this.

"Miss Kitty! I have to leave, please come back."

I feel like my heart is being ripped apart. I can't breathe. I have to leave and I have no choice but to leave her behind. How can I live with that choice? This is more than I can bare. Why won't she come back to me? She has to be so close. She seemed happy on the truck. What could have happened to cause her to not want to come back?

As I walk away, I start to cry. Deep, heart wrenching sobs pour out. I can't stop. This can't be happening. I can't bare it. I'm not sure I'm even capable of driving. I can barely walk up the hill to the truck. I know it's over. I have lost her for good. I just pray she finds a good home and nothing bad happens to her.

As I pull out of the truck stop, I look over to where she was, hoping to see her before I am too far away. Nothing. I don't see any movement in the brush or anything. This just can't be real. It was so great having her on the truck with me and I know she liked it too. I will never forget her. I have a lot of good memories and pictures to remember her by. Why? Dear Lord, why?

Is there really a chance this load will get swapped and I can come back to look for her a little more? Do I dare hope? This is more than I can bare, Lord. Please help me, I can't do this on my own.

Chapter 18

~~

I FINALLY HAVE A load back to Dallas. It's been three weeks; Thanksgiving is over and I have been hauling Christmas stuff. It's all the same stuff really. It starts at the beginning of October and goes till somewhere around New Year's then it starts all the candies for Valentine's Day. Does it matter? Nothing matters much anymore. The loads can rot as far as I'm concerned. I don't even want to go back to Dallas. Why? It's just a reminder of what I've lost. Maybe I should have refused the load.

She is gone. She might have gotten ran over, there's so much traffic in Dallas. She might have gotten picked up by the pound, there are so many cats there, they can't tell me if she is or was there or not. There is no way she would still be at the truck stop and I have no way of searching for her.

Dear Lord, should I stop to check? Be with me and keep my heart from ripping in two. I'm going to go ahead and stop at the TA when I get into Dallas. You know I only have half an hour to spare. If she is there, please, please send her to me or I will know for sure she is gone and I will never look for her again or go back to that truck stop again. Thank you, Lord.

There it is, maybe I should just drive on by, it hurts to even look at it. No, I prayed so I will stop. I won't stay long, I can't. I will just stop to fuel and check one last time. That's it.

Oh my gosh, Is that a cat over there? Could it possibly be her?

"Miss Kitty? Is that you?" No, that cat is way too small to be her, it looks like a kitten. I don't think it's even the right color. Is it? If it would just stay still, maybe I could tell. It's crouched down so low, it's too hard to tell. How could that possibly be her? I'm letting my imagination run wild. This hurts so bad. I should never have stopped here.

"Miss Kitty, is that you?"

Meow.

"Miss Kitty?"

Meow.

Oh my gosh, she is coming towards me crouching down low with her belly to the ground. That can't be her. That cat is so small. So skinny and frail. It looks like the wind could blow it away. I think it's starving, it looks half dead already, poor kitty.

Meow. Meow. Meowowl.

Oh my goodness! That is Miss Kitty! Thank you, God, Thank You! It is her! Poor baby. She was here the whole time? Dear Lord God, thank you for sending her back to me. Thank you for watching over her. Please let her be alright. Don't let her be hurt or sick and don't let her die on me now. Thank you so very much, dear Lord.

"Oh, Miss Kitty! I have missed you so much! Let's go back to the truck. I put out fresh water and food just in case I found you."

Meow.

Would you look at that? She jumped right back up there like she had never been gone. She is starving. I can't believe she was waiting all this time for me. Thank God, I found her. Thank you, Lord.

"Don't eat too fast Miss Kitty, it'll make you sick. Don't drink too much water all at once."

Purr, purr, purr.

"I love you too! How I have missed you." I just can't believe I found her again. My heart hurts again but this time I think it's joy, relief, happiness and a little disbelief. Thank you, dear sweet heavenly Father, thank you.

"I just have to hold you for a little bit, you can eat all you want in a minute, let me just hold you."

She is back just int time. I have to get this load to the receiver; I'm going to be late if I don't hurry. I can't believe she is back. Thank you, Lord.

We get to the gate and I'm sure I must have tears in my eyes. I try to wipe them away so no one sees.

"*I see you on the schedule right here, go ahead and get in door 112. Don't forget to check in at the office once you are docked and chocked.*"

"Thanks."

This will take a couple hours to get unloaded, I need to hold Miss Kitty again.

Purr, purr.

"I love you too. You can tell me all about your adventures, I just need to hold you for a minute."

Purr, purr. Mew, meow.

"I'll have to tell everyone I found you. They have been so worried and so very sad too."

Won't Babygirl be happy. Everyone else will be too, of course, but I think it hurt her as bad as it did me when Miss Kitty left.

I think I'll stop at a Wal-Mart or find a pet store to try and find her something really special. She is so picky I don't know what to get but I'll find something. I wonder if they have a special treat she would like? Maybe a new toy? A new pillow for the window? A new bed? Something to climb? A new scratch pad? I'll have to see what I can find. I'm overjoyed to have her back on the truck with me.

She seems so happy to be back. She grabs a bite to eat then rubs on my leg and grabs another bite. I don't see any sores anywhere and she doesn't seem to be hurt. I guess God sent an angel to watch over her. He had to have protected her or she never would have made it for so long by herself.

"We have to go pick up the next load, you are going to be good to the guard, right? No getting out here. I just got you back and I can't take a chance of you getting out again right now."

Mew.

She doesn't mind checking in with the guard as long as they allow her to sniff them. She didn't get too close to the window, just close enough to get the slightest whiff and that was good enough. She seems a bit shy or scared to let anyone too close to her. People probably treated her badly when she was left for so long. Was she searching for me? Did she try to find her truck?

"No jumping out when we go to scale. I hope you learned your lesson on that. I can't stop to love on you right now but we will be stopping for the night after we get the load weighed and get down the road a little way."

Meow.

We have to go to Michigan; they need this load there by noon on Christmas eve or they won't have anyone there to unload it until two days after Christmas. This is another urgent holiday load, we will have to hurry if we want to make it in time. We don't get holidays off unless we can't get the load delivered on time then we get charged a fee for not getting there in time.

I think they are sending us to Boston after this load, I hope we get to pick up the chocolates in New Hampshire after that, they always give free samples to the drivers. A lot of samples, not like Hersey's, they don't give the drivers any samples at all. Not that I need them but it sure makes a driver feel special. A lot of places have doggie treats at the gate but nothing for kitties. I'm hoping if I go to the same customers often enough, they will start having kitty treats at the gate. That would be awesome.

Lord, thank you so very much for bringing Miss Kitty back to me and keeping her safe while I was away. You created all the animals so I know you have to love animals. Thank you for loving Miss Kitty, thank you for sending her back to me. Thank you for sending her to me in the first place or I never would have known how truly special she was or how much I needed her. Watch over us and protect us and please don't let her get out and run off where I can't find her ever again. Thank you, Lord.

Chapter 19

I KNOW WE ARE in a hurry but I think I can spare just enough time to stop here in Texarkana to grab my mail. I can park at the yard and take my car down really fast. Maybe I can grab something for Miss Kitty at Wal-Mart while I'm right there. It shouldn't take too long.

Back on the road. Dispatch sent a message after I pulled out of the yard asking why the truck is showing being at the yard. I was gone before they noticed. I did tell dispatch thank you for getting me to Dallas and that I did find Miss Kitty and she is back on the truck with me. They were shocked. They had already given up on her, I'm so glad I didn't. Well, I almost did but I'm glad I didn't.

I got Miss Kitty a wobble toy that has a feather on top. It has a battery so it makes a little bit of a humming noise when it wobbles and she hates it. She jumps over or around it but won't even get close to it. I'll have to find someone with a kitty to give it to. I think some of the animal shelters take toys as donations, maybe I should see if they want some of the toys Miss Kitty doesn't want.

It looks like an accident here on I-40 in Little Rock, I sure hope we don't get hung up too long, I'll get chewed out for taking the time to stop in Texarkana for sure then. I don't think they are coming to a complete stop. Good deal, we might get through without too much of a delay. The traffic is just horrendous. Everyone wants to be somewhere for Christmas so the highways are jam packed with cars, trucks and even RVs.

Here we go again, slowing down. I wonder what's going on in Memphis, the traffic looks backed up for miles. Good thing I cut off on I-55 right before the backup. I would hate to be held up by a parade or something.

Wow, there's hardly any traffic on I-57, is that a good sign or bad one? You can't tell this time of year until you get right up to something. Let's hope there is nothing to get right up to. It's just so strange after the amount of traffic we have had on all the other interstates. I don't see much of anything.

It was too much to hope for, not having to deal with traffic. The closer to the holidays, the worse the traffic gets. As soon as we got to I-24, the traffic was so bad we were only able to go about 45 mph. This is not good. We cannot miss our appointment. I don't want to be stuck sitting at a ware-house on Christmas.

They still haven't fixed the merge of I-57 onto I-70, what a surprise, not. They will probably be working on it for the next 5 years. Thankfully we don't have to stay on I-70, it looks like a nightmare. Nothing but cars lined up as far as you can see. I hope I-57 North past here isn't as bad as this.

I like stopping here at the Petro in Effingham, they have food right at the fuel island and a big parking lot. It's not that junk some of them have at the fuel islands, it's actually decent food. They have the iron skillet inside and a decent store but I don't have time to go inside right now.

I don't mind this part of Illinois, it's actually kind of pretty. I just don't like Chicago. I hope I don't get held up by any of that traffic when I get off I-57 onto I-80. I don't have to go into Chicago but the traffic from there gets pretty bad and backs up I-80 quite frequently. My friend Sasha lived in Chicago for 11 years and she said Chicago is actually really pretty and there are so many things to do that I would love it. I have driven through there for years and never have I found anything pretty about it.

This is more like it, as soon as I came off I-80 onto I-94 heading North, I could feel the peace starting. Not that they don't have traffic, they do but it doesn't feel so hectic here. It's a calm feeling. Is it just the change of scenery or is it something more that gives it that extra beauty? I could see living here. I don't know if I could stand the winters here with the lake effect storms but I still like it. In the summer it's so beautiful and looks so green and lush. I wish it was summer right now.

We finally made it. We even got here a little early, what do you know, I had plenty of time. No worries about having to sit here waiting till after

Christmas to get this load delivered. It is a blessing that they all wanted to go home as quick as they could, they had my truck unloaded in no time. I was unloaded before the actual appointment time and on the road to get the next load which will keep us rolling.

It's the little things that count. We are able to stop and have a real Christmas dinner, not just what groceries I have on the truck. The mom-and-pop place we stopped at gave all the driver their dinner for free. A lot of truck stops charge like $25–$30 for the holiday meals. I think we pay it so we don't have to cook for ourselves and we don't have to be alone. It's nice to be with fellow drivers on a holiday even if we aren't family, we are all stuck out here together.

Every now and then we see familiar faces. They might not be friends but just that you have seen them on the road from time to time and it feels like you know them just a little. We don't often talk to each other but on a holiday, you can walk up and talk to anyone of us and we will most likely smile and stop to have a little conversation. We all miss our families and even a smile can make a big difference.

Thank you, Lord, for all you do for us out here on the road. Thank you for keeping us safe and allowing us to have a wonderful dinner for free this year. Thank you for the drivers we met and the wonderful people who gave us the dinner. Thank you for loving us and sending your son into the world to show us your perfect love. As always, thank you for protecting us in all our travels. Thank you, Lord.

Chapter 20

"MISS KITTY, DO YOU want to come out here and check out the snow? It's a cold but some kitties like to play in it." Plop. "How do you like snow? HaHaHa."

She stood in it for 5 seconds not moving, lifted a paw and shook it, then she jumped right back into the truck. I really need to find her some kitty boots. They made a movie about "Cat in Boots" right? OK, it was a cartoon but they should make boots for kitties. Her poor little toesies got too cold. I bet other kitties feel the same way. We should make a Miss Kitty line of clothing and accessories for kitties.

The roads weren't too bad driving up here but there is snow everywhere. I stopped here at the rest area between Pennsylvania and New York to see if Miss Kitty wanted to get out for a minute or two. She hasn't gotten out much since the incident. I'm very thankful but I worry she will feel trapped inside if I don't let her get out a little. I stay right with her; I'm not just opening the door for her anymore. I would try the harness and leash again but she still seems a little traumatized, so am I, it can wait.

The roads are supposed to get worse, especially in and around Buffalo. Thank you to all the people who wished for a white Christmas, I have to drive through that while you sit home by the fireplace all dry and warm drinking your hot chocolate, visiting your families. My family is over 2,000 miles away and I'm up here trudging through what makes all you people happy for Christmas. While you're wishing for that white Christmas, could you please wish for the roads to stay dry? That's my Christmas wish.

Miss Kitty is getting better, I don't know how else to put it. She was literally skin and bones, she didn't weigh anything at all when I picked her up. I don't think she would have made it much longer out there. She stays right by me all the time but when I get out to do my pretrips, she runs back to the bunk. She hides every time it rains and loud noises scare her. She doesn't even look out the window that much. If I pass a truck, she freaks out when she sees it beside us and runs to the back. Very rarely does she jump up on the dash. She doesn't even want her pillow up there anymore.

If I had a house, if I didn't have to drive all the time, if I could stay at home with Miss Kitty, if...that's all I can think about sometimes. If... Life isn't easy and I have to do what I can to survive just like everyone else. So what if I don't have a little house on a little piece of property paying someone else to live in a place they own, going to work at someone else's company so that they become rich and I make just enough to survive. That isn't what life is all about to me. I live in a truck, sure, but I don't just go to work and come home to the same old thing all the time just barely making it from paycheck to paycheck. I don't pay rent but my truck payment is probably twice as much as rent. I have enough to pay my bills and enough to share with my family. As an extra bonus, I'm out in the world, seeing things most people only see in pictures or on tv. I get to see the things they can only dream about seeing.

Have you seen the statue of liberty with your own eyes? I have. Actually, the first time I saw it, that was very disappointing, I can't brag about that. I was driving over the bridge into New York and there was this little green thing in the river. I stared at it thinking, there is no way that is what I think it is. The statue of liberty is huge and it's like in the ocean or something right? No, it's right here in the river. That just doesn't look right. The point being, I see things other people just wish they could see. This is my house, it moves, it takes me to the most amazing places. I can't always get out of the truck to see things up close or check them out but I do get to see them with my own eyes.

Most people have never been inside a cave before. I have driven an 18-wheeler into caves. Some are small but others are like a highway through there. They have lanes painted on the ground, stop signs, red lights, one-way areas and everything, like on the above ground roads. Some you barely go in and the docks are right there. Others, who knows just how far they go. Some say there is one running the length of the entire country underground. I don't know if that's true or not. The farthest I have gone in one was three miles. Yep, three miles to where my dock was. It didn't end there, that's just where my dock was. Take that, you cubical dwellers.

If I was working a regular job, living in a regular house, I would have to leave Miss Kitty at home alone every day while I went to work. I couldn't bring her with me. She would never get to sniff the air in all the different places and meet all the different people even if all she does is sniff them. She really loves to smell everything. How would that be a better life for her? She loves traveling and she loves that I am with her all day, every day. She is never alone for very long on the truck. She doesn't like being alone.

Miss Kitty might not want out in the snow but I think I see a smile on her face. She might have enjoyed getting to have the experience even if she didn't enjoy doing it. That makes sense to me. At least she knows what snow is and knows she doesn't want out in it. She lost so much hair while she was gone, no wonder she likes staying inside the truck, I keep it around 68 degrees year-round. Most people try to argue with me that 70 is the perfect temperature but that's too hot. If you do any physical activity at 70 degrees, you are sweating, at least I am. That's too hot. To each their own. Miss Kitty agrees with me. I think. She does go get under the blankets or at least the pillows sometimes.

"Ok Miss Kitty, you've had the chance to sniff the cold air, see what snow is and be out of the truck for a whole 5 seconds. That's a good little break, right?"

She hasn't spoken to me much since that first couple days when she meowed and meowed at me trying to tell me how upset she was that I left her and how thankful she was that I came back. She will be ok, I know it.

Lord, thank you again, for bringing Miss Kitty back to me and thank you so much for protecting her while she was out there alone, by her lonesome. Keep us safe as we travel down these snowy roads. Thank you, Lord.

Chapter 21

"IT'S SNOWING AGAIN MISS Kitty. Do you think it's ever going to stop? I don't want snowed in out here on the highway. We might need to get off the road for a while. At least until it stops snowing, I can just barely see the road. We aren't really getting anywhere going 30 mph anyhow, we are just wasting all our drive hours." This seems a little early in the year for this heavy of a snow storm. It's getting a little too dangerous for my liking. They have a Petro just up the road a little farther. Almost there.

Whew, I'm so glad we stopped. I went ahead and fueled up, just in case. After I parked, I walked in to see if they knew how bad the roads were ahead of us and they said they just got off the phone with the highway department and about 40 miles up they had the road closed. They have a few motorists they are trying to rescue, so it is worse down the road. They also informed me that the road is closed behind us as well. Apparently, we would have been caught in the road closures if we hadn't gotten off when we did. Thank you, Lord, for giving us a place to stop.

So much for being down South when the snow hit. I wanted to go visit my friend in San Antonio where it's nice and warm. Let all the newbies get their winter driving experience in up here. I had plans to ask for a Southern route for the winter so I wouldn't have to mess with all this. I forgot all about it when Miss Kitty went missing. It's a bit late to ask for that now. I'll bet a lot of drivers had the same idea and there probably aren't any Southern routes left.

The Southern routes are mostly California to Florida and back. There are some Georgia loads mixed in there but it still keeps you out of the snow.

A little ice and wind in a few spots but very little snow. I wonder how long it's going to snow before it lets up? This doesn't look good.

***

Wow, there is almost a foot of snow built up on my truck already. I don't think it's letting up, I think it's getting worse. It might be time to call dispatch and let them know the situation. This is not good.

"It looks like you are taking a long break, did you lose that cat again?" Dang dispatch, they know better than to bring that up with me. It's too touchy of a subject right now.

"No, she is all nice and cozy in the truck with me. It looks like this break might last all night. You should check the weather board."

"All night? You don't have all night. What are you doing? Celebrating New Year's with friends? You better not be drinking on the truck. You better not be partying instead of driving. Are you going to get this load there on time?" Dispatch seems to be in a foul mood today.

"It's not New Year's yet and I don't drink. There is a reason for this call, did you check the weather board yet? If you haven't, you better do it now."

"Holy cow, I saw that it was snowing this morning but I didn't expect this. Looks like all the roads up there are closed. You are off the road and in a safe location, aren't you?"

"Of course. I just wanted to let you know why I'm not rolling. That's all."

"Thanks for the heads up, I'll let the customer know what's going on. I'm sure they already know, looks like the roads are closed there as well. Stay safe and call me if you have any updates."

"Will do."

Click.

The roads are also closed where I deliver this load? Just how bad is this storm? I saw the snow warnings but I didn't check to see how bad it was going to get or how long it was going to last. I just didn't care. We might be here a while, now I care. No way am I going to try to get back out there on the road and get caught in a road closure without a place to park. It's a good thing I fueled up as soon as we pulled in, I'm going to have to keep the truck running and we definitely don't want to run out of fuel if this is turning into a blizzard.

***

I had to go inside to the restrooms and I swear the snow was almost to my knees already. This is bad, I mean really bad. The cell service is getting spotty, I might not be able to use the phone much longer. The tv uses internet so that's out. I have movies on DVD and I have a few shows downloaded on the tablet, we shouldn't get too bored. Let's hope I don't need to go back inside for anything or I might have to dig a tunnel through the snow just to get to the building.

***

During the summer it looks a lot like Colorado up here but their winters are sure a lot worse. I don't think I have ever seen this much snow at one time before. I don't need to step out to see how deep it is, it's over the bottom of the door which is about chest high. It snowed all night long. I had to get out to clear out some space around the cat walk so the exhaust could get out earlier and I noticed the snow isn't building up under the trailer since it has the skirts on it. What a relief, I won't have to dig the tires out and that will help keep the exhaust from coming into the truck and suffocating us. There is no way I'm getting out of the truck again in this weather. Nope, not for anything. Well, unless the exhaust builds up and does start coming into the truck but nothing else.

***

It's still snowing. Where is it all coming from? How can it still be snowing? It's not snowing hard anymore but it just amazes me that there is any snow left in the sky to fall. I don't know how many feet that makes but it's almost up to the window on the truck. That's too deep for me to get out in, I can't even open the door. No way Miss Kitty could get out there, she would be buried under the snow so deep I doubt I'd be able to find her.

***

I have been trying to keep the windows cleared off as much as I can so we can keep an eye on what's happening out there. We saw the snow plows go by a few times; they go in groups of three. The lead one was the far inside lane by the median, then the middle one came behind him and finally the last one was in the lane by the shoulder. I don't know when the roads will be open again but we are NOT in a hurry to get out there in this. We might be here another night. I don't dare shut the truck off, I might not be able to start it again and who would be able to help me if all the roads are closed.

***

They came through to clear the local roads bright and early but totally blocked the entrance and exit for the truck stop. I guess that's their way of keeping the trucks from leaving just yet. That's ok guys, I'm in no hurry to get out there. They are still running three plows down the highway periodically. I think the snow has almost stopped but I have no way to get my truck out, I'm buried in here. By the looks of it, all the other drivers are too. You can only see the top half of the trucks; it looks so funny. I know it's not a laughing matter but it looks so wrong it's hard not to.

***

Some of the drivers have started digging their way out of the trucks and going inside. They are letting drivers use the snow shovels they keep around for cleaning the parking lot in order to clear around the trucks. I spent quite a while trying to get out of my truck and now, I'm working on digging the truck out.

***

Finally, I made it inside to see what was going on with the roads. I never stopped to wonder about the people working in there. I found out that they have been sleeping on the seats and the floors in here. They couldn't leave either. I feel bad for not even thinking about the workers here, they live right around this area, so what was I supposed to think? They drove home when all the roads were closed and somehow made it back in the next day to work? Their cars are completely buried. I guess because I didn't see them, I just didn't think about the people who work here. They must have had it so much worse than the drivers. At least we have a bed to sleep in.

***

I let the snow stay on the windshield this whole time because it was like having a layer of insulation. Now, I kind of regret it. Because of the heat from inside, the snow thawed and turned to ice. A thick layer of ice. I got the snow off and am trying to defrost the windows to get that ice melted. I dug around the truck and cleared enough out from in front of me that I might be able to get out of here. They opened the roads up a little while ago but I feel exhausted from all that digging to get the truck out, I'm not quite able to drive just yet. I can't right now anyhow, not until I get these windows cleared off.

***

We made it out after being stuck for three days in the truck stop. This was one heck of a storm. I'm taking it nice and slow out here. They did a good job of keeping the snow from piling up too high on the road in most spots but I heard they had to send people out to dig out the plows a few times. The roads are still a little icy but not like they would have been if everyone would have been allowed to drive on them and packed the snow down. If they could have even driven at all in this. The spray they put on the roads helps keep it from icing back up as the snow melts. I'm still going to take it easy. I'll get there when I get there, I just want to get there in one piece.

Having this delay has been good for Miss Kitty. We spent a lot of time together and she realized I wasn't going anywhere and wasn't going to leave her again. She started to play with one of her little balls and scratched her scratching pads. She even jumped up on the dash a few times but the windshield was too cold so she didn't stay up there. Since I didn't have to drive, I could give her my full attention. I think she really needed that.

Slowly but surely, we are getting there. I got hold of dispatch again finally. I told them not to set an appointment, I would get there eventually and that would have to be good enough. They said they can't reach the customer right now so just do what I can and we will worry about it when I get there. I wonder how bad they got it? I hope we don't get shut down again.

***

We have finally made it to the customer. I tried to get checked in but they informed me that half the workers still can't get in to work and with it being New Year's they are short on workers for other reasons. They will try to get me unloaded today but can't promise anything. They let me go ahead and park in the dock to wait. I won't open the doors until they are ready to unload me of course but I'm so thankful I don't have to leave and try to find somewhere to park around here until they are ready for me. Boston is not a pretty sight right now.

I need to go shopping pretty soon, I've used most of the supplies I keep on the truck. I would have gone shopping at the truck stop but the prices are about three times what they are in a regular store. I don't know whether the products cost them more or they are just taking advantage of the drivers because they know we can't get into regular stores very easily.

***

I did have to wait overnight but they got me unloaded bright and early this morning. Dispatch didn't book another load for me right away because they didn't know when I would get this one delivered so these guys were nice enough to let us stay parked here until dispatch was able to find another load. We are getting ready to go get it now. I've been checking the road and weather very carefully; I want to make sure I know what to expect before we leave this time.

Lord, thank you for protecting us and keeping us safe and warm through the storm. Thank you so much for allowing us to find a good place to park and get off the roads before they got really bad. Thank you for our having enough food and supplies on the truck to last us through it all. Thank you, Lord.

Chapter 22

I THINK DISPATCH FELT sorry for us, they gave us a load heading South where it's warm. We did get to pick up the chocolates and get our samples. I love the samples. Miss Kitty didn't get any samples. I need to figure out how to get them to give her treats, even if I have to give them the treats to give to her. She gets excited when we pull up to the gate, she wants to greet them and sniff them but they don't have any treats. They give the doggies treats; I think she is jealous. One of the guards offered her a doggie treat once, she seemed a little offended but she wasn't rude, she just jumped back over to her seat and looked back at the guard with her nose in the air.

Miss Kitty is starting to get some of her snark back. She has started sitting in her seat again and even wanted the window open so she could sniff the air in New Hampshire. That storm brought a lot of healing to her, I think it might have been sent from above. I don't doubt for a second that God cares about animals, after all he created them. Animals can have unconditional love where humans lack the ability to give much of anything to others let alone love.

I can feel the temperature warming up, maybe it will be warm enough to let Miss Kitty out of the truck for a little while. She hasn't shown an interest in it but then again, we have had nothing but snow lately. It might be time to work with the leash again, that way she won't go running off. I don't think she will do that again but let's not take that chance right now. She has been extremely cuddly; I hope she doesn't lose that. It's the best feeling in the world to kick back and watch a movie while your kitty snuggles up with you.

"Miss Kitty do you feel like getting out of the truck? We can try going for a walk. Are you ready to try the leash?"

Meow.

"Let's just put this on."

Hiss.

"Calm down, I don't want you outside without it."

Hiss.

"Miss Kitty, calm down and be good, let's put this on."

Hiss.

Maybe it's too soon. Do I dare let her out without the leash? I'm a bit scared of going through that again. I don't want to traumatize her by forcing her to put the harness and leash on but I'm a little worried about just letting her out without it right now. Do I dare let her run around without it? I have to trust she won't run off, she found out what it was like out there by herself.

Miss Kitty is staying right by me, maybe it'll be ok. Uh oh, they are letting their dogs out and no leashes. I don't have room to talk, Miss Kitty doesn't have a leash on either right now and I'm little afraid she will get scared and run.

"Come here Miss Kitty. I can carry you, just stay calm." Good thing I left the door open, she let me pick her up and that's when the dogs saw her and came running, she jumped down and ran. She ran right back to the truck, jumped in and waited for me. She didn't run off. I think she is going to be fine.

Maybe she will do a pretrip in the morning with me. I miss when she would walk around the truck with me. It was as if she knew just what she was doing and what to look for. Baby steps, she is doing great.

Tap, tap, tap…tap, tap, tap. "Miss Kitty? What are you doing up?" TRRRR. "Never mind, I guess you know what time the alarm is supposed to go off. Let me get the coffee going." Scratch, scratch. "You want to do the pretrip with me? Give me a second."

Meow.

It's chilly but at least we are out of all that snow. Miss Kitty ran around the truck doing her pretrip and jumped back in letting me finish. Her pretrip was a bit short but she did do one with me, we are making progress.

Thank God for coffee. My brain just doesn't want to wake up this morning. I'm trying to read the directions the customer has about getting into their facility so I don't have any problems when we get there. I read them but they weren't making any sense until the coffee kicked in. We have to pass the main plant, go two blocks and turn right, between the hardware store and the car lot, cross the tracks, make another right and come in the back gate. I hope they have a guard at the gate back there so I don't end up in the wrong yard. There should be trucks and docks and hopefully a sign. Why are they vague about stuff like that? They might think they are giving a lot of detail but for someone who has never been there, it's rather confusing. Especially before coffee.

***

We found the place without too much difficulty but they sure are putting my backing skills to the test. This yard is very small and they have a lot of trailers packed in here. It took a bit for me to figure out how to get the truck maneuvered through their yard and get backed into a dock. I think they ought to try to find a bigger facility, there not room for them to expand on this one in the middle of town.

Some companies grow too big, too fast to keep up and some have been around so long, the town grew around them blocking them in. How do you know how much space you will need when you start? You don't know for sure how big your company will grow. How much extra room do you plan for? What if you don't have the money get enough space? What happens when you need to expand and you can't? I don't even want to know how some companies get started in big cities where they can't get enough room to begin with, how do they grow their business?

Miss Kitty isn't impressed with this place either. She wanted the window down at first but as soon as she took a sniff, she jumped down and went into the back. Usually, she likes to watch when we pull in and dock. The people here aren't rude but they aren't friendly either. Everyone looks very busy, I'm just glad I don't have to work here, no one even has a smile.

Our next load takes us to Houston, we might be able to buy some of my favorite coffee while we are there. The grocery store we are going to has their own line of coffee and it is better than any of the fancy coffee shops can offer. I don't like paying $8 for a cup of coffee when I can get a whole bag of my coffee for less than that and one bag lasts a couple weeks. I better stock up; I don't get through very often and I tend to run out long before I can get back through. Most store brands are lame at best but not theirs. They have the absolute best coffee I've ever tasted.

I can't wait to get back to the warm weather and dry roads. This has been the opposite of fun playing in the snow and getting buried in it. I'm so relieved to be out of it, I sure hope we never do that again.

Lord, thank you for sending us somewhere warm to thaw out for a while. Let it stay warm and dry. Thank you, Lord.

Chapter 23

"Is your nose getting darker Miss Kitty? Is it bruised? Did you bump it? Are you hurt?" Her nose has always been so pale pink it looks white. Do cats' noses turn colors?

"Let me look at it."

Hiss.

"Miss Kitty, let me look at your nose."

Growl.

"You aren't going to let me at least look at it?"

She snapped at me. I can't believe she actually tried to bite me.

"Fine, I didn't want to see it anyway."

I might need to keep an eye on that just in case. I don't think it's anything to worry about, maybe it's a little scratch or something. It's not bleeding or anything, maybe it will go away.

***

The winter hasn't been too bad this year other than being extra cold. After that blizzard we went through early on, we haven't seen a whole lot of snow. I have refused three loads going back up to the Northeast. They finally stopped trying to send us back up there. They hate it when I refuse loads so they try to give me crappy loads as a punishment. I don't want them to know it but I actually like some of those crappy loads. They are usually around 500 miles and deliver the next day. Guess what, I get one after another and another one and before you know it, I have more miles at the end of the week than I would with those long runs.

Most of our loads have been across I-40 which keeps us pretty much below the snow line. A little in Flagstaff now and then, maybe a bit here and there across the country but Oklahoma seems to get snow and ice even if the states before and after it are dry. I swear there is something weird about that state. We have been very fortunate not to have to chain up. It's not hard, just a hassle and I prefer not to if I don't have to. I can wait till the road gets cleared. I can't always do that but if I can find a safe place to park, it's worth it. In the time it takes me to put the chains on, drive extra slowly while they are on and then get them off, they usually have the roads plowed and sanded.

"Miss Kitty, let me look at that nose of yours! It's getting darker and I don't think it's a bruise. Get back here. You can't run from me and I know all your hiding spots. Come here and let me take a look."

Growl, hiss.

I'm getting a little worried about Miss Kitty's nose. She won't let me look at it unless I grab her by the neck and hold her long enough to see it but she fights me. She bit me a couple of times, I just want to help her. If it continues to get worse, I am going to have to take her to see a vet, I don't know what's wrong or how to do anything for it.

***

It's supposed to be Spring but I think someone forgot to change the dial. It is still way too cold out here. I think I'm going to request a load to Florida so we can get as far down South as we can for a little while to thaw out. Thank you, Lord, for allowing us to keep South and not have to go back up North this winter. I didn't request it but did hint strongly that I would like to stay South if possible.

It's been days and Miss Kitty's nose isn't getting better. I don't know what it could be but it's getting so dark it looks almost black. I made an appointment with the vet but I have to get this load delivered and get back to Texarkana before we can see them. I don't know what kind of medicine she needs but I have some cold sore ointment I bought for my lips when they were getting chapped and cracked so I think I'll try that on her nose. I don't think it will hurt her. She looks so uncomfortable.

***

Guess what? Shock of all shocks, the cold sore ointment worked on her nose. Is that how kitty cats get cold sores? On their nose? It started clearing up right away. She didn't want me touching her nose at first but I had to try something on it. She bit me the first time I tried but I got it on there. I called the vet and they said if it was cleared up, there was no reason to bring her in. They said as long as she doesn't have any side effects from the ointment, it was fine to put it on there. I'm so relieved.

"Do you feel better Miss Kitty?"

Purr, purr.

"See, I was just trying to help you. Do you feel bad for biting me now?"

Purr, purr.

I'm so glad that's over with, I don't have enough Band-Aids on the truck to keep trying to treat her. The Band-Aids being for me, of course. I can tell she is all better, she wants loves and cuddles again.

Thank you, Lord, for healing Miss Kitty. The ointment might have played a part but I might not have thought about using it on a cat. Thank you for giving me that idea so she could get that cleared up.

'Tis the season for colds, fever blisters and flu. Please don't let Miss Kitty get sick Lord. I'm one of the fortunate few who don't get sick very often. I don't know if kitties do or not. I don't hear people talking about their cat getting a cold. Do they carry antibiotics for pets in the store? Can you keep it around just in case you need it or does it go bad? Do you have to get a prescription from a vet every time like you do from a doctor when you get sick? Should I try to find a jacket for Miss Kitty?

I really think they need to make more stuff for cats. There are all kinds of stuff for dogs. Everyone says just get stuff for a small dog and it's the same thing. That is not true. Cats aren't built quite the same and they move differently than a dog. They jump and climb so it might have to be something stretchy but still needs to keep them warm. You would think someone would have figured something out by now.

Chapter 24

~~

I<small>T'S</small> <small>TIME TO GET</small> back to see the kids, it's birthday time for the grands. I try to get to town about the time school gets out and the birthdays begin. Not all of them are the end of May, beginning of June but that's the easiest time of the year to get there so I do a huge birthday bash for everyone no matter when their birthday actually is. It's the first time I get to visit Colorado after the winter because I avoid coming between January through April. I try to arrange some big party and a fun event for the kids and hope it's something the adults will participate in too.

Me and Miss Kitty are planning to stay with Babygirl while we are in town. Miss Kitty hasn't stayed at anyone's house overnight before. There are three other cats there, I hope she can make friends with them. Or at least be civil to them. Here she comes now, I guess we will find out soon.

"Hey Babygirl, thanks for picking us up. Let me load Miss Kitty's cat box in the back so it doesn't get knocked over. I brought her own food, I'm not sure if she will eat your kitties' food. She is a little picky about that. I'll grab a couple of her balls, maybe she will like playing fetch with the kids."

"We have been looking forward to your visit so much. The kids are thrilled Miss Kitty will be staying with us. And you too of course. That's all they talk about." Babygirl sounds so excited.

"I have missed you guys. Let me get Miss Kitty in the carrier, I don't want her jumping out and getting lost. She is getting quite used to the carrier."

"I'm so glad you found her again, I think she learned her lesson."

"Let's hope so or you will have to find her and take care of her this time."

It took a few minutes to get everything loaded up. I just realized the kids weren't in the car. Bad gramma. I should have noticed right away.

"Are the kids still in school? I thought they were out already."

"No, they are getting the house ready. I figured it would be easier to just come by myself since they would just fight on who gets to hold Miss Kitty on the way home."

"Good idea, fighting bothers Miss Kitty. How do you think your cats are going to handle having her stay there?"

"I think they will be ok; they go outside a lot."

It's funny how a car bothers Miss Kitty but the truck doesn't. She doesn't like being in the carrier while going down the road but even when we are in our own car and I don't have her in the carrier, she just goes and finds a spot to hide. I don't get the big difference. It must be a cat thing.

"Miss Kitty! I've been waiting for you; do you want to come to my room and play?"

"Miss Kitty, you need to come to my room, I set you up a bed and everything so you can sleep with me."

"Miss Kitty! I love you! You need out so I can love on you!"

"Miss Kitty! Are you going to be my kitty now?"

"Quit crowding her and I will let her out. You are going to scare her if you all try to grab her at once. I will introduce you one at a time so she can sniff you and remember who you are. It's been a while since she has seen you."

"I want to be first!"

"No, me first!"

"Hand her to me Gramma, she loves me."

"I want Miss Kitty"

Oh my, I hope they don't start fighting, Miss Kitty might not like any of them if they do. I better make them line up and find a place I can sit and hold her while I introduce each one.

"Alright Miss Kitty, it's time for you to say hi. Do not bite anyone! Let me hold you for now, I'll let you down after you greet everyone."

I made Babygirl organize the kids and bring them to Miss Kitty one at a time. She sniffed and let them touch her but she wouldn't allow them to grab or hold her. I think they were pretty disappointed but I told them we would be here for a whole week so they would have plenty of time to hold and pet her.

Luna was the first cat to meet Miss Kitty. That went as to be expected with a bunch of growling and hissing but thankfully, no fighting. Pumkin was next. She took one look at Miss Kitty and ran. Miss Kitty took that as an invitation and chased her. Back and forth through the house they ran and the kids loved it. TT finally got her chance and decided Miss Kitty was going to be her best friend but Miss Kitty didn't agree with her. They ran through the house but the only one growling or hissing was Miss Kitty.

At bedtime everyone wanted Miss Kitty but of course she wanted to sleep on top of me. The kids tried to steal her throughout the night but she climbed under the covers with me. A couple of them tried lifting the covers to get her but after a bit of growling and hissing, they gave up and went back to bed. Not a restful night for me but it went better than I expected.

Miss Kitty has decided, if she is going to be here, she is going to get everyone in line. There is just too much activity and noise for her liking. She swipes at the kids' legs if they are running, gets in between them if they are arguing and hisses at them when they do something she doesn't approve of. Shas even started training Babygirl. If she raises her voice to the kids, Miss Kitty jumps at her and nips her leg. Not hard, it's not a bite, just scrapes her teeth across her leg. The cats have given her a wide berth and stay outside the majority of the time.

***

I went shopping today and when I got back to the house, I couldn't believe what I was seeing. The chair Babygirl always sits in was occupied by Miss Kitty. I looked around the living room and everyone was sitting on the couch all quiet and reading or playing on their tablets.

"What is going on? Babygirl, why aren't you in your chair? Why is everyone so quiet?"

"*Shh! Don't be so loud Gramma, you might upset Miss Kitty.*" It was said with such earnest reverence I started to laugh.

"Babygirl, why aren't you in your chair?"

She points to her chair. *"She won't let me sit there."*

I laugh even harder. This is just too much to hold back.

"She can't keep you out of your chair, she is a cat, you pick her up and move her."

"Nope." Her face is totally serious and the kids are looking at me like I am the crazy one.

I'm laughing so hard I can hardly breathe. I can't believe she has everyone walking on eggshells around her.

"Just try to move her, she hisses and tries to bite you. If we make too much noise, she starts to growl then makes this scary howling yowling noise like she is getting ready to attack." One of the kids informed me.

That does it, I have to sit down before I fall down. This is hilarious. I pick Miss Kitty up and set her on my lap and what does she do? Turns around and stares at everyone. No one moves, everyone looks so nervous. I can't stop laughing. She now rules the house and everyone in it. What a cat.

***

I was able to take everyone to Banana's amusement park for the big party. There were about 30 of us all together. The kids played all day, the adults ran after the kids trying to watch all of them, I sat back and watched it all. I think everyone had fun. Next time I'm bringing Miss Kitty to help keep everyone in line.

This has been great. We all had fun together, went out to eat a lot, played games and watched movies. My son's kids were upset Miss Kitty didn't get to stay with them but I assured them next time we would stay there. I'm not ready to leave and Miss Kitty isn't ready to give up her throne but dispatch has a load for us so we have to say goodbye for now. We will get back through again but it will probably only be for short little visits until next year around this time.

It's hard to leave. Everyone is out here to say goodbye. I had to wipe a tear away a couple of times. Miss Kitty looks sad too. She finally got everyone in line and we have to leave. Who is going to be the boss now that she is leaving? I think if cats could cry, she might have. Every single one of the kids has to hold and pet Miss Kitty, she is going to be covered in tears and snot, she better not jump on my bed to clean herself off. My son and his wife made me promise we would stay with them the next time we are here.

Lord, thank you so much for such a loving family. So many families never find the time to get together and they have drifted so far apart. Please keep this family together. We might not see each other as often as we would like but we still love one another so very much. Thank you, Lord, for such a great visit this year. Keep everyone safe while we are apart. Thank you, Lord.

Chapter 25

I HAD THE BRIGHT idea to move my bed to the top bunk and store all our stuff on the bottom so we could get to it easier. I've slept on the top bunk plenty of times before, it sounded like an excellent idea. Well, it wasn't. I'm now laying here in the floor, in a puddle of everything you don't want to think about, while Miss Kitty stares down at me.

I can't move just yet and there is no way I'm calling out for help. I don't want anyone to see me like this. Who could help me anyways? The doors are locked and I can't move. I think I will just lay here a bit longer until I can breathe again. I hurt everywhere. I grabbed the hand grip while falling and might have dislocated something. I fell right on the potty and broke it so now; I'm lying in that too. How humiliating. I hope no one ever finds out about this.

My blankets, which fell with me, are all soaked, I'm soaked and Miss Kitty is still looking at me. Is she laughing? Here I am laying on the floor in pain and she is laughing. I have to get up, clean this mess up and take a shower. I'm going to have to disinfect everything and do laundry before we leave here. I am definitely moving the bed back down to the bottom, I do believe I have learned my lesson.

All I did was roll over; I swear the top bed is half the size of the one on the bottom. I didn't even realize what was happening at first. I was on the bed and then there was no bed. My brain could not process that in time and down I went. Did I say any bad words? Lord, forgive me if I did.

***

This is quite a task to undertake first thing in the morning. I'm slowly getting it done. I'm still pretty sore. Most of everything is cleaned up so I just have to get it all put back to where it should be. What on earth is all the commotion about out there? I need to haul this stuff out to the trash so maybe I'll be able to find out what's happening while I'm out there.

"Aahh! Get it out!" A guy screams as he comes flying out of a truck.

Did I just see a cat jump out?

"Someone get me a stick, there is a critter in my engine."

There it was again. I think it's going from truck to truck down the whole line. I think I see it. Crap, that driver opened the door and it jumped in. I'm pretty sure that's a cat.

"Aahh! There is a wild animal in here. Help!"

Yep, that is a cat and it looks just like Miss Kitty. Oh no, I better find out before someone hurts her or it.

End of the line, if it will just stay there a minute so I can get to it.

"There you are. Miss Kitty? What are you doing out here?" It is Miss Kitty. I've been so busy cleaning the truck up, I forgot that I had the door open so I could throw things out, I didn't even realize she was missing. I reached the last truck in the line and she was sitting on the cat walk looking at me.

"Time to get back to the truck. I'm sorry it was such a mess; did it scare you? I almost have it all cleaned up." I think it just scared her a little. Did she think I was moving out and abandoning her there? Poor cat, she didn't know what was going on. It's been a rough morning for both of us.

"Is that a cat? It was just a cat? I thought a wild animal had jumped in my truck. She is kind of cute."

"Awe, it was just a kitty cat. I'm glad I didn't hurt her."

"That couldn't have been a cat in my truck, it looked vicious like it was there to eat me, she isn't big enough to hurt anyone."

"What's all this about? Is that a cat? What's it doing in a truck?"

We finally got back to the truck and Miss Kitty jumped from my arms into the truck to inspect it. It's still a mess but it's clean now. Did she go to find me help or to tell the other drivers how dumb I was? Tattle tale.

Maybe she will calm down and relax now that she knows I'm ok and I'm not moving out of the truck. It might have scared her when I fell and then again when I started throwing stuff outside.

Lord, please don't let anyone find out about this. Please help me to use my brain before doing things. Thank you, Lord, for not letting me break my neck. That would be a horrible way to go.

Miss Kitty wasn't trying to run off, she didn't try to hide from me or anything. She acted like she was looking for something, maybe she wanted a different truck. Surely, she wasn't looking for a new mom. I try to keep her happy. I buy her things, try to spend as much time doing things with her as I can but bad things happen and things tend to upset her when she is confused about what is going on. I'll try to stay calm, even if I fall off the top bunk in the middle of the night.

I don't plan on doing anything like that ever again for sure. I just hope Miss Kitty isn't too upset, I don't know what she must have thought about it all but she got out of my way while I was cleaning. Good in a way, bad in so many other ways. I really do wonder if she was trying to find me help or something. The good thing is, she didn't run away. I am so thankful for that.

Thank you, Lord, for keeping me unharmed in my fall. It could have been so much worse. Thank you for watching out for me and keeping Miss Kitty from running off. Thank you, Lord.

Chapter 26

BACK AND FORTH ACROSS the country we travel. There is no fear of not working, everyone needs food to survive and they need us to bring it to them. Talk about job security, everyone has to eat, what better job security is there than bringing the food they need for survival to them? We don't always haul food but we do always haul something people need for daily life.

I don't worry about doing my part to help my neighbor or pay it forward or whatever they say these days. Every load I haul helps individuals as well as entire families. It might not be out of my pocket directly but I am contributing to the welfare of humanity. It sounds important when I say it like that. So many people treat truck drivers like they are worthless, don't they understand how important we really are? We are the reason they have food on the shelves when they need something. We bring everything they buy, not just food. The clothes they wear, the shoes, the jewelry, hats, coats and whatever else they put on. The list can go on forever. From the car they drive, to the house they live in, everything had to have at least the building material brought in. Furniture, decorations, appliances all these things get shipped by truck.

So why do truck drivers have such a bad rep? Someone please explain that to me. I'm not saying we need special treatment but people act like they actually hate truck drivers. I for one think that is so unfair. We work more hours and hardly ever get to spend time with our own families. How do you change peoples' minds about something like this? Afterall, it's been this way forever as far as I know? How did it all start? Did something happen that made such a bad impact that the world decided to hate every truck driver out on the road? I really don't understand.

Miss Kitty loves being a truck cat. She shows off for people and loves to get her picture taken. I can't actually let her out of the truck to interact with them, she doesn't like them up close and personal. She doesn't want petted, just admired. So far, the only people, other than the family, she has let pet her have been mechanics. She loves to get greasy and they seem to find it irresistible to help her with that. I can't give her a bath on the truck but I do keep baby wipes on hand so I can help her get the grease off. I don't think she needs to be digesting all the grease from cleaning herself.

I need to stop and stretch my legs for a bit, sitting all the time isn't good for a person. What do office workers do? They can't just get up and walk around any time they feel like it. Is it hard for them to sit there day after day? I did work briefly as an accountant before I started driving but that was years ago and all I remember is that I was miserable. I stared at the computer entering in numbers till my head was ready to explode. I'm so thankful I was able to get away from that because I enjoy so many things out here on the road.

This has to be the prettiest rest area I've ever seen. How have I missed it all these years? I must have stopped here before. If so, why haven't I been back? Is it new or did I just forget to visit it for so long? I think I would have remembered this. It's amazing. There are hand crafted rocking chairs and little tables to sit and relax. It's so green and peaceful and the butterflies are brilliant bursts of color here and there, the birds are singing such a soft and sweet song. The flowers are in bloom and it smells heavenly. If I had a hammock I would gladly live here. Is this Tennessee or North Carolina? No matter, I would love to stay in a place like this. Not in a rest area but like to have a backyard like this if I had a house.

I find these little places every now and then. I forget where they are or something, I guess, so I don't stop very often, just drive on by and then one day I stop and it's like a dream. If I find them at the right time of year, it's like finding a piece of paradise. It's so great when I have the time to really enjoy my surroundings. I can let myself relax, see and feel the beauty God has created, let my mind stop worrying about all the details of life, just let things drain away for a while.

Miss Kitty let me put the leash on her and we actually walked around to the back together. When we got back here, she flopped. That's ok, I flopped in one of the rocking chairs myself. We are both flopped, just enjoying nature. Miss Kitty watched two squirrels playing and I thought she would want to chase them but nope, she just watched as they ran across the yard and up a tree, back down, over to another tree, up that one, jumped from the branches of that tree to another one. It was so fun to watch, Miss Kitty twitched a few times but just laid right there by my feet. Even she needs a day off the truck just sitting peacefully, watching nature.

We have been running pretty hard these past couple weeks. That's good, it gets us caught back up from all the money we spent while we were visiting the family. It's wonderful going for a visit, it just drains the bank account so we have to work a little extra hard to make up for it. That's why we live out here. If we took too much time off, we wouldn't be able to do things like the birthday bash week or any of the fun stuff throughout the year with friends or relatives across the country. How could we visit everyone throughout the year if it wasn't for the loads going through? I try to see everyone I can at least once a year even it's just long enough to grab lunch on the way through. It's a good thing I don't have too many relatives or friends, I might not be able to afford that.

I wonder if we had a house somewhere and weren't driving all the time if anyone would visit us? We wouldn't be able to travel to see them very often, would they travel to come see us? Some of my relatives haven't see each other in years. A lot of families are like that. Everyone is so busy working and when they do get time off, they can't afford to travel to visit family, especially if they live too far away, let's face it, families aren't close anymore. Some cousins have never even seen each other, some don't even know who they are related to. I know I have a few I have never seen.

Wow, look at that gorgeous sunset. That is truly a work of art. Did you create that just for us, Lord? Thank you. I love you too. The perfect ending to such a lovely day. This is nice. I almost dread getting back on the truck. Sometimes I wonder if I will ever be able to get off the truck and have a house of my own. What would it be like to live in the same place all the time? Would I get bored and want to move after I was there for a while? Could I be content to stay in one place? Where would that place be? What kind of a house would I want? I don't think I'd like an apartment with neighbors so close and so much noise all the time. I guess I'll figure it out when or if the time comes.

Thank you, Lord for another day. Each day is a gift, thank you for today, Lord.

Chapter 27

I'M SCARED. NO, I'M terrified. My whole right side is completely numb. Not tingly or any other feeling, there is absolutely nothing at all. Is this what a stroke feels like? Am I going to lose my mind or be trapped here in my head for the rest of my life? Am I going to have a life to have the rest of or is this the end? Am I supposed to do something? What do you do when you are having a stroke? Shouldn't I have been prepared for something? How do you prepare for something like this?

Am I supposed to call an ambulance? Can I even make a phone call? Can I speak? "Hello, I might be having a stroke, can you help me?" I can speak. Or am I only thinking I can? I've heard that some people think they are speaking clearly but all anyone hears is gibberish. How am I to know?

"Miss Kitty, can you understand me?" Oh my gosh, I didn't think about what is going to happen to Miss Kitty. Who is going to take care of her if I'm in the hospital? What if I die? Who is she going to live with? I should have made plans for her in case anything like this happened. What am I going to do about everything now? I need to call the doctor. Good thing I already made my coffee early this morning before I had a stroke. I need coffee right now.

Wait, if this is a stroke, I won't be able to drink my coffee, that could tell me if it's a stroke. Let's see if I can get my cup with my left hand, grab with the right, it's moving. That went ok, let's see if I dribble coffee all over myself when I drink. Not even a drop. I might not feel my face but it seems to be working enough to drink coffee. I've seen what happens when peoples face gets paralyzed and it's not pretty. How do I hold things if I can't feel anything? My arm is moving, is my hand working? I can't tell if I'm actually holding the cup with my right hand or not, let's not find that out right now. I don't want hot coffee all over me.

Ok, time to make the call. Maybe. I'm scared. If it's not a stroke, what is it? Are they going to want to run a bunch of tests on me? Do I just go to the hospital or call an ambulance? I need a shower before I go get a bunch of tests ran. How do I take a shower when I can't feel anything on my right side? Am I going to be able to walk to the showers? What if I collapse in the shower? That would be so embarrassing. Maybe I should try standing up in the truck first. Hmm, I can stand up, let me grab the shower bag and maybe I can take a shower before I collapse. I can call the doctor after that and see if he wants me to go to the hospital. I'm so scared, what are they going to find? Will I ever be able to drive again?

I think I might be losing my mind. Pull it together, first things first, I need a shower. Let's see about getting that much done. We will worry about everything later unless something else happens, if so, I can worry about it then. I'll just take things slow and hope for the best.

Lord God, please help me. I'm really scared. You have promised never to leave or forsake me. I need you now. I don't know what's happening and I don't even know what I'm supposed to do. Be with me Lord.

Whew, climbing out of the truck when you can only feel one leg and you aren't sure if the other leg is even going to hold your weight is quite a challenge. Not only did I manage to get out of the truck and inside the building, I was able to take a shower. The strangest thing happened as I was showering, I started getting some feeling back on my right side. I'm still scared half to death but I can feel things and I can move. I have to call the doctor. I have been putting it off long enough. Just do it!

"Doctor Bill's office, how can I help you?"

"I need to make an appointment. As soon as possible please."

"What seems to be the problem?"

"When I got up this morning, I sat down to drink my coffee and everything on my right side went completely numb. I was afraid it might be a stroke or something so I would like to see the doctor to see what he has to say."

"*Why didn't you go the hospital immediately? You need to hang up and dial 911.*"

"I think it might be getting better, I was able to move around, sip my coffee without it running out of my mouth and even take a shower. I just need the doctor to tell me if it's all better or if I need some kind of medicine."

"*Oh my gosh, you need to be in the hospital. I don't understand why you didn't call 911 immediately. The doctor doesn't have any openings for over a week. Please, go to the hospital.*" Said a panic sounding receptionist. Why is she panicking? I'm the one who might have just had a stroke.

"I'm actually a little afraid to go to the hospital so can you call me back if you have any cancelations? Please. Thank you."

Click.

Maybe I should have called 911 but if this is nothing serious, I would feel like a fool for panicking and freaking out. How do you know if it's serious enough to need the hospital? I don't want to go to a hospital unless I know for sure it's something serious. Isn't your doctor supposed to tell you when something is serious enough to go to the hospital? That's why you see a doctor instead of rushing to the hospital for every little thing.

Ring, ring.

"Hello?"

"*This is Doctor Bill's office, is this Tory?*"

"Yes, this is Tory."

"*I spoke to the doctor and he is very upset with you. He can't see you right away but the RN can. She wants to know if you have someone that can bring you down here or if you think you can get here by yourself. She has an opening right now and can get you in but she is booked for the rest of the day.*"

"I think I can drive myself. I'll be there as soon as I can. Thank you."

Click.

Well, time to find out if I can drive or not. I'm not numb anymore so as long as it doesn't happen again, I should be fine. I hope. Lord, don't let me lose control as I'm driving and please don't let me hurt anyone else on the road. Thank you, Lord.

I made it. Thank you for helping me get here safely, Lord, and let them find what's wrong with me.

"Hi, my name is Tory and I have an appointment with the nurse."

"Yes, she has been expecting you, she wanted me to bring you back immediately."

She leads me back to the exam rooms.

"Right here, go in and change into the gown please, I'll let her know you have arrived."

"Thanks."

I am so nervous. What is she going to find? Is it serious? Is it going to happen again? Am I going to need surgery? What is taking so long?

"Tory?"

"That's me."

"Tell me what's going on."

After I told the nurse everything that happened this morning, she had me go to the back room to get x-rays done on my neck. What the heck is going on with my neck? Why would they need x-rays? I'm waiting for someone to come tell me what's going on. They said they don't have anyone here who can read the x-rays right now so I'm just waiting for someone to tell me something.

How long am I supposed to wait? If something was wrong, wouldn't they have seen it right away? Why do they need to have someone read the x-ray to them? Does this mean it is serious? Where are they? Do they know I'm back here freaking out? Can't they send someone back to at least check on me? It's been almost 45 minutes and I'm really getting scared. What exactly did they see?

"Tory?"

"Yes, are you the one who is going to tell me what's going on with me?"

"No, I'm sorry. The person who knows how to interpret the x-ray isn't in today. There is another place you can go if you need answers today. You will have to pay for it all yourself, they want cash up front and they don't take your insurance."

"Oh, I would really like an answer to what is wrong with me so where do I go and who do I need to see?"

They are 'The Imaging Company' and they are just down the road.

"Fine, give me the address and I'll go there. I think I need answers right away so I know if I can still do my job."

So much for seeing the doctor. Maybe I can get some answers from these guys.

"Hi, my name is Tory and I need to get some x-rays done on my neck. The nurse at the Doctor Bill's office said she would call ahead to arrange it for me."

Yes, we have everything all set up for you. We do need you to pay up front, we don't deal with any of the insurance companies here.

"That's fine, I was prepared for that."

***

Blast it all. Yes, they got me right in, yes, they took the x-rays and then do you know what they had the audacity to tell me? They didn't have anyone to read the x-rays so they sent them over to Doctor Bill's office. What happened when I called Doctor Bill's office? They said they had received them but I would have to wait for someone to read them. I got a little upset so I went back in to The Imaging Center and asked why they hadn't given the x-rays to me and they said they couldn't. I explained how I had paid for them out of my own pocket, they should belong to me. They told me I should go work something out with Doctor Bill. I even told them what Doctor Bill's office said, they didn't care.

So, now I am waiting again. I'm not freaking out anymore, I'm rather upset. They want me to call back in three days. Three days and I'll be over a thousand miles away. If it's not serious enough to tell me what is going on then it must not be serious enough to keep me from driving. I told dispatch to get me a load first thing in the morning. This was all for nothing. Why should I worry if not even the doctor is worried?

***

It has been over a week and I have called the doctor's office every other day trying to get the results. I was finally told I need to find another doctor. Say what? They can't even tell me what's wrong with me? Why do I need to find another doctor? Ugh. I might never know what they found out with the x-rays but I refuse to freak out over it again. The only thing I know is it most likely has something to do with my neck. If anything like this ever happens again, I will find a doctor who will let me know what's going on, at least, I hope. Until then I'm not going to worry.

I have no idea what I'm supposed to do in a situation like this. I feel fine so I'm going to go on as if nothing ever happened. Unless they restrict my license then there is no reason I can't drive.

Lord, you are the God of healing, please heal me. I don't know what's wrong but you do and you know how to fix it. Thank you and forgive me for not turning it over to you from the beginning. It did me absolutely no good to see a doctor. I'm not sure what this was all about but please forgive me. Help me to put my trust and my faith in you, Lord.

Chapter 28

"MISS KITTY? WHAT ARE you doing? What are you playing with?"

She has something underneath her but she won't let me see it. She is purring at it.

"Are you just going to lay on it? Let me see what you have. Why are you trying to hide it from me?"

It looks like a fuzzy ball but I could have sworn I saw it move. Where would she have gotten a brown fuzzy ball? I buy her the bright colored ones so I can find them easily in the truck.

"Eek! Did you bring a mouse onto the truck? Do you know what they do to trucks? They eat the wires and everything else. Get it out now! Don't just lay there and purr at it!"

She is purring while laying on it. Does that mean she likes it or is that something she does before eating something.

"Just what were you thinking? You don't bring critters into the truck. We have talked about this before. Get it out of here."

Purr.

"Miss Kitty, get that mouse. You are not going to keep a pet mouse on the truck!"

Purr.

We have chased the mouse all over the truck. Me, to get him off the truck, Miss Kitty, to play with him. He is in hiding and I'm at the store getting a mouse trap. Do you have any idea how many different kinds of things they have to get rid of mice? What works best in a truck? I can't have any poisons. I feel like we are having a repeat of the fleas but on a bigger scale. The fleas were horrible but the mouse can actually do serious damage to the truck. If she wants a friend on the truck, I can get her a cat friend.

Here is one that captures them and traps them inside so you don't have to see the dead mouse. I don't want to kill the poor thing but I can't have it eating the wires or anything else on the truck. It better not get into all the food on the truck. I'm going to have to check all of it and throw away anything he might have gotten into. Ugh. Dang cat. Don't they eat clothes too? What if it has built a nest in my clothes? Can you wash them and be done or do I need to throw away my clothes too? Sigh.

"I found a trap Miss Kitty, where is your mouse? No, I did not get a cage to keep him, I got a trap so we could get rid of him. If you want a pet you will have to find something that doesn't cause damage to the truck."

Where could he be hiding. I have checked and sealed all the food. I went through all my clothes. Please don't be under the dash in the wiring. The traps are set, I feel bad for the poor thing but there is no way we are keeping a mouse. We are going to have to have another discussion on what is acceptable to bring in the truck and what is not.

***

I heard him last night making little mouse noises and I also heard Miss Kitty chasing him but it soul=nds to me like she is just playing, she isn't hurting him or trying to eat him. The traps were empty and there were no mouse pieces laying around. I guess that means he is still here somewhere. Why? Please Lord, help me get the mouse off the truck. If you want it to live, let me find it and get it off the truck or when he gets hungry and the only food is in the traps, he will have to die.

Miss Kitty has acted all innocent today. I am only giving her a little bit of food. If she gets hungry, she can eat the mouse. It better not bite my toes while I'm driving. I haven't seen it but I know it's in here.

***

I can't stand going to bed another night with the mouse on the loose. Just what am I supposed to do about this? I've been checking the traps but he hasn't tripped any of them. Is Miss Kitty sneaking him food? I've double checked and he can't get into anything by himself, she has to be feeding the mouse her food. Crazy cat, why would she do that?

I smell mouse urine, it's getting strong, the mouse has to be found, he has to go one way or another. This is too much. Miss Kitty needs to do her job not make a friend. Lord, please help me. Let me find it or let it be in the trap so I can get it off the truck. Please, Lord.

Finally! I found the mouse in my shoe this morning and dumped him out. He survived and ran off to find another home. Thank you, Lord. I believe it must have been your will for him to live so as long as he is not on my truck, I won't be the one to kill him. Thank you, Lord, for letting me find him so I know he is off the truck.

Chapter 29

SUMMER IS ENDING, I can't believe how fast this year is going. It will be over and a new year will start. It seems like time works differently for me. Or maybe just out on the road. It's not the same out here. Didn't this year just start? So much has happened you think it would be just the opposite and be dragging on but maybe because so much happened, time flew by.

We are here at the yard in Texarkana and I went in to take a shower, I thought it would be ok to leave the door open for Miss Kitty so she could get out and play. I like to park at the far end, away from all the other trucks and anything Miss Kitty doesn't need to get into. She can't go too far since it's completely fenced in and she gets a little more freedom to roam. We even have guards at the gate that keep an eye on her for me, they think she's so cute. She has been known to go visit the mechanics at the shop, they adore her. At least most of them do, I think there might be one or two who might not but they aren't mean to her.

When I got back to the truck, I found a bunch of feathers inside. They were small feathers so it must have been a small bird. I didn't see any other signs of a bird or birds.

"Miss Kitty? What is going on in here? Did you have a party or what?"

I did a thorough search of the truck and found Miss Kitty hiding but no bird or bird parts anywhere. That was a relief, I thought she might have tried to get her another pet on the truck. I don't know for sure what happened but with her hiding, it must have been bad. She likes chittering at them but she never really chases them and she is terrified of the big ones.

I have seen birds chase her. That is the only explanation I can think of. There are quite a few feathers, how many birds were in the truck? There are too many for it to have been just one. This looks rather suspicious; it makes me wonder what exactly did go on while I was out of the truck.

I came to town to get my mail and do a little shopping. It's also time for Miss Kitty to get her annual shots in order for her to be on the truck with me. It helps that the washers and dryers at the yard are free, that saves me some money when I do laundry here. My car is parked here at the yard so I can do all the running around town that I need to.

I'm actually here at the yard for another reason as well. I have a lump under my jaw that is growing. It's just a little worrisome because it's getting a bit tender. I'm not in real pain or anything but I thought I might need to get it checked out. My previous doctor won't see me so I have been searching for a new doctor. Texarkana is divided in the middle so half the town is Texas and the other half is Arkansas. My insurance is in Texas and most of the doctors I have found are on the Arkansas side. My insurance won't allow me to use a doctor on the Arkansas side. That makes it a little difficult.

I'm not too worried, this is probably no big deal, I just wanted to get it checked out. I found a doctor willing to see me so I set an appointment right away. He had a cancellation today at 2 pm. That's better than I hoped for. He will probably just give me a prescription for antibiotics and send me on my way. I'm sure that's all I need.

Not good. The new doctor looked at the lump and said I have to go to a specialist. He said because of where it's located, I'll have to see an ENT doctor. There is only one on the Texas side, Doctor Kutz, and I can't get in for three weeks. I'm sure it's nothing. I need to let dispatch know that I have to get back here in three weeks. They are probably going to put me on the Tyson loads, won't that be fun. I don't hate Tyson loads, just the waiting to pick them up bothers me. They almost never have the load ready and it takes forever for them to load it. And, it stinks. Really bad. Oh well, it keeps me rolling and the money coming in.

***

Miss Kitty loves Tyson plants. I have to keep the window rolled down the entire time or she throws a fit. She would dearly love to get out and see where all the smells are coming from but they forbid any pets out of the trucks here. I wonder if they would consider free samples for the pets? I'm not sure if Miss Kitty would even eat raw chicken and I'm not sure I should ask them. Would Miss Kitty want it raw or cooked? She doesn't like people food so I would assume she wants it raw. I've never given her raw meat but I hear that's what cats need. I don't think I have the nerve to go ask them for raw meat for my cat. There is a chance they might not object but it just sounds wrong to me.

"Miss Kitty, what are you doing? Get back in here."

I can't believe she climbed out onto the mirror. I grabbed her as quick as I could. She was going to jump down from the mirror. She could have been hurt jumping from that height. Cats don't always have perfect landings, no matter what people say.

"Miss Kitty, we need to talk about the rules again. Unless I open the door for you and keep it open for you to jump down, you cannot, let me repeat that, cannot get out of the truck, especially when we are at a customer's yard. They don't allow you out of the truck here and don't want you getting into things. Do you understand that?"

Meow.

"You have to follow the rules or we will get kicked out. They won't let pets in here at all if they won't stay in the trucks. Then we would never be able to get loads from Tyson again. You don't want that do you? Just stay in the truck and everything will be fine. I won't roll the window down for you if you try getting out. I think you have lost at least half the privilege of the window. It stays most of the way up till we are off their yard."

Meow.

"What are you doing now?"

Meow, merowl.

She is jumping from the seat to the dash and back to the seat over and over. It almost sounds like she is chittering to a bird between her strange meows but a little different. I didn't see any birds back here, up by the docks but not back here.

"Is that a chicken? It must have escaped. No, you absolutely can't go chase it. Calm down."

Miss Kitty thinks she needs that chicken. What is she going to do? Bring it on the truck as a pet? That's what she tries to do with other animals. No, not happening.

"Miss Kitty, settle down, you can't play with the chicken. I'll try to find another kitty for you to play with but you are not getting a chicken. What would you do with it? It's too big to eat and you can't chase it on the truck, there isn't room."

Merowl. Mew. Merowl.

She is determined to get that chicken. They better get the load done or I'm going to have to leave.

"Enough! Settle down and stay in your seat young lady. You can not have the chicken and that is final."

***

It's a good thing they got the load finished so we could get out of there, it was driving Miss Kitty nuts and she was driving me nuts. She was so convinced she needed that chicken. Does she need more toys? I have bought her literally every toy they carry at the stores and she won't play with anything but those fluffy balls with the shiny spike stuff all over them. What am I to do when she doesn't like anything I buy? She does seem to try to bring her own pets onto the truck. I'll see what I can do about getting another cat for her to play with, maybe she is just lonely.

We are heading to California again. At least she has never tried to bring a fish on the truck. What on earth would I do if she did? No, that's too much to think about right now. I'll have Babygirl search online for toys and stuff. They should have something I haven't already tried.

Lord, please let me find something for Miss Kitty. She needs a toy or a friend or something to keep her from being bored or lonely and I have no idea what to do for her. Thank you, Lord.

***

The trailer had a flat tire this morning. No surprise, I think I have to get a trailer tire repaired every other week on the average. I did run into a friend of mine in Amarillo while I was getting the tire fixed. I was able to have lunch and catch up with him on what has been going on in his life. I think he is a year younger than I am and I found out he had a heart attack about a month ago. I couldn't believe it; he always seemed to be in such good health. He was skinny and could eat anything without gaining an ounce when he was a kid, I guess that caught up to him. He is doing alright now he told me but that is a scary thing for me to hear. I feel so bad for not even knowing what he went through. He told me he had to have bypass surgery.

That goes to show, anything could happen to anyone at any time. As the bible says, we are not promised tomorrow. I am a horrible friend to have, I never keep in touch with anyone unless I'm going through an area they live and have a little time on a load. I don't call or send messages or whatever people do to keep in touch with each other. I need to do better if I want to have any friends at all.

How do you have friends when you are never around? What do you talk about when all you do is drive and they actually have a life and get out and do things? I drop into peoples lives for a brief moment and am gone again. It's like I just get glimpses of who they are. Is that even considered a friendship? It's not an excuse but they could call me anytime to keep in touch but they don't. Makes me wonder what friendship really means. I call people friend all the time but how much do I really know about them? I almost never see any of them. Once every year or two or more in some cases doesn't make a very close relationship.

That's too much to think on right now. It was a hard reminder how short life can be and how we need to keep in touch with those we care about. That's enough, that's all I can do.

Lord, help and heal the sick and hurting tonight. Keep them safe and show them your love. Keep our hearts sensitive to those around us and thank you for the friendships of the people you have brought into our lives. Thank you, Lord.

Chapter 3Ø

THEY HAD A SPECIAL event where they do pet adoptions in front of the store where I went to do my shopping so I stopped outside and saw the most adorable kitten. There was an $80 adoption fee but she had all her shots, spayed and even chipped. My thinking was to bring her on the truck and let her and Miss Kitty get to know each other so Miss Kitty would have a friend. It's one thing to introduce two cats if you have a home and they can avoid one another until they are ready to get to know each other but I discovered the truck is too small to give them that time and space.

I felt so bad taking the kitten back to the store the next day, I let them keep the adoption fee and apologized for traumatizing the poor thing. I don't think I will ever attempt something like that again. They ran and jumped and broke things and clawed and scratched and bit and it was a harrowing experience. Literally the only way to describe the events of the night. I had to go back to the store to get bandages and return the kitten to a safer environment. Yes, I might be limping slightly today. Miss Kitty will not be getting a kitty friend, at least not one I pick out for her.

***

Miss Kitty loves the smell of California and I'm happy to say, she did not try to bring a fish onto the truck. We did get close to the ocean in Long Beach but weren't able to get to the actual beach thank goodness. She doesn't like water so I think it would have been safe enough, I'm just not brave enough to find out. She will have to find something acceptable on a truck or be the only pet on the truck. Period.

***

On our many travels, through the many places we go, I have tried to stop to enjoy somethings along the way. Today we had the privilege of stopping at a little town in Kentucky. We got the load delivered early and had some extra time so we took a three-hour break. I don't think people realize how beautiful Kentucky is. I don't hear very many people talking about taking a vacation here. Why? It's absolutely gorgeous. We found such a nice spot under the trees to have lunch.

It felt like we stepped into a medieval painting or something. We parked in a little hide-a-way so no one could see us and we couldn't even see the road with all the traffic. The trees grew overhead in a canopy sheltering us from everything but allowing the light to shine in somehow. It felt like a magical little spot hidden from the world as if it only existed for us. It had a surreal feel to it.

Miss Kitty ran around sniffing everything like she had never smelled anything like it before. She took off running a couple times but I couldn't see anything she would have been chasing. She would stop and run back the way she came and lay there for a minute then get up and do it again. I think she was just having fun and getting some exercise in. If I could fit one of those cat wheels for her to run in onto the truck, I would buy her one. I think she would like that. I don't know of any way to get one on the truck even if we took stuff out.

***

Ugh, we are heading back to California. Miss Kitty might like it but I really hate the traffic and only being able to drive 55 mph drives me nuts. Someone really needs to change those speed limits for trucks. I am convinced that is the reason there are so many truck accidents in California. People weave in and out of the trucks as if they aren't even there half the time but it's the other half that is the problem. No one wants to drive 55 so everyone tries to pass the trucks and end up hitting each other or slamming on the brakes and getting hit by the truck.

***

A load to Missouri next then it's back to Texarkana to see the ENT doctor. Maybe the loads will run late and I won't be able to keep the appointment. The lump is getting a little sore but that could mean it's just healing, right? Am I falling apart? Is this what happens to people when they get older? If it is, I don't like it and don't agree to the whole aging thing. I'll happily remain this age for the rest of my life. I think Miss Kitty would be fine with that as well. The whole nine lives thing doesn't actually extend their lifetime. I don't think. Does it?

***

I really like stopping at the Petro in Oak Grove, they have so many things for the truck in the store. I buy a lot of my t-shirts there and they have a BBQ restaurant at the edge of the parking lot. I love pork ribs. I buy them all over the country but I do believe Texas has the best, I'll have to continue doing research on that. I never know what I will find in some of the strangest places.

I found some of the best chili at the fuel island of the Petro in Laramie Wyoming. As it turns out, the lady working there has her uncle ship it to her. Apparently, he is a gourmet chef in Chicago and sends bags of frozen chili to her and she sells it there in the fuel island. You can't buy it in the iron skillet, they would have to add it to their menu all across the country. I personally think that would be awesome, it's the best chili I have ever eaten. It's shocking where you find the best things, not where you would expect, that's for sure.

I don't know what Miss Kitty likes best in the places we stop. Does she have a favorite? I know she loves the smell of the ocean but what else does she enjoy? I try to pay attention to the places she really likes but I sure wish she could speak better English so she could tell me.

***

We picked up the load for Texarkana today. I feel like the time went by too fast. I wish I could swap out with another driver. I could say, "Oops, I forgot I needed to get back there, I'll just change the appointment and get back some other time, no big deal." I can't do that, I know that. I am just a little nervous. I know it's going to be fine; I just don't know if I'm ready for whatever it is if it's not fine.

***

Well, I just got back from the ENT, Doctor Kutz; he looked a bit concerned. He did a biopsy and wants me in next week for a bunch of tests. I told him I was a truck driver and couldn't take off every week so he said I could push it off for two weeks but he really needed to get the tests done. He will call me with the results of the biopsy.

I am not going to worry. Not in the slightest. I'm going to pretend nothing is wrong and that will be that. I can't let this get to me. I have informed dispatch I will probably be needing more loads through to do whatever I need done but I am not quitting and I won't be taking a whole bunch of time off to just sit around and freak out about this, I need to keep working. I refuse to panic before I even know what is going on.

Lord, I know you are watching over me, please keep me calm and at peace while I am waiting to find out what is going on with me. I tend to stress out over the small things and I can't afford to do that right now. Let everything be ok. If it be your will, you can heal me and I won't have to deal with any of this. Your will be done, not mine. I know there is a purpose for everything. Thank you, Lord.

Chapter 31

~~

I REALLY HATE HAVING to get back to Texarkana so often, how am I going to make money out here? Being on Tyson loads all the time really sucks. Miss Kitty doesn't seem to mind but I do. I tried to discuss this with dispatch but they are convinced that keeping me on Tyson is the only way they can have the control over the loads they need to bring me back in when I need to see the doctor. Isn't that just wonderful. I guess it's not too horrible, I know where almost all of the plants are so at least I don't get lost.

Doctor Kutz called concerning the results of the biopsy. He believes it might be cancerous. This is not the result I was looking for. What am I going to do now? He said they needs me to get the tests done and do a consult on a treatment plan. I can't do treatments and still be able to work. What about Miss Kitty? How am I going to take care of her? Or rather who is going to take care of her? I know I should have had this figured out by now but there is no one I know of who could or would take care of her.

No, this can't be happening, it's not real, it's not possible. Does this mean I'm going to die? Dear God, please don't let me die, I'm not ready. How long do people live when they have cancer? Maybe the biopsy was wrong. He used the words "We believe we have found a cancer cell". Does that mean there is a chance it's not? How can they not know for sure? What exactly did they find?

I don't think I want to go back to have all those tests ran. If they are positive then it makes it real. I don't want this to be real. I know I can't pre-vent it by ignoring it but I'm not ready to acknowledge it right now. How does a person willingly go have test ran when they know the outcome is very likely a death sentence?

Dear Lord, please don't do this to me right now. I can't handle it; I have so much I need to do still. I have a family counting on me for help. I have grandbabies I need to watch grow up. Why is this happening to me? Please heal me so I don't have to go through this. I'm not strong enough. Do you have a purpose in this? Is there a reason I need to go through this? Is it a punishment for something? I'm scared Lord. Please be with me through this. I can't do it alone. Thank you, Lord.

***

"What are you doing Miss Kitty? Are you herding that squirrel to the truck? No, don't you dare try to get a squirrel in here. We have talked about this multiple times. No pets, no critter allowed in the truck."

The squirrel agrees with me and ran under instead of in the truck but now it's under the truck doing who knows what kind of damage as they race back and forth on the frame. How am I supposed to get a squirrel out from underneath the truck?

"Miss Kitty, leave the squirrel alone."

Oh my gosh, are those other squirrels heading over here? Are we going to be attacked by a bunch of angry squirrels? Do they all stick together and attack like a mob? I've heard they have a pretty vicious bite. What is she thinking?

"Miss Kitty! Get back in the truck, his friends are going to get you!"

I can hear them running under the truck. How on earth am I supposed to get them out? I can't climb under there. Maybe I can use the broom to get them out. Or at least scare them into coming out. Maybe if I just slap it on the ground a few times.

"*What are you doing?*" Oh no, someone sees me. This must look pretty strange.

"Nothing much, just trying to get a squirrel out from under my truck."

"*Why do you have a squirrel under your truck, they usually stay away from the trucks.*"

"My cat decided to play with one and herded it back to the truck. I think she wanted it to go into the truck but instead it ran under the truck."

"*I see, so you are out here slapping a broom on the ground hoping to do what exactly?*"

"Scare them out. I can't climb under there and they are too busy with the chase to listen to me so I though if I made enough noise, it would scare them out."

"*Just a minute, I have an aluminum bat in my truck. That should be loud enough to scare them out.*"

I don't think they are paying that much attention to us because they are still running around under there.

"*Hey, what are you guys doing out here? You are making enough noise to wake the dead.*"

Another driver, great, we're going to cause so much attention someone is bound to call the cops. I can't wait to explain this to an officer.

We have an audience watching and some of them are laughing at us. How rude. Then again, I bet we do look pretty silly out here slapping the ground all around the truck with a broom and a bat. They probably don't even know what's going on yet. It does seem pretty ridiculous.

"Miss Kitty, get out here and bring the squirrel with you. Enough is enough young lady."

The crowd seems to be enjoying the show. Some of them spotted the squirrel and was cheering it on while others spotted Miss Kitty and started cheering her on. I just wanted both of them out from under my truck. I wouldn't doubt if a few of them didn't start placing bets. I thought I heard them whispering about the outcome. With all the cheering it is difficult to tell for sure.

There goes the squirrel, I hear a few people booing for Pete's sake. I'm thrilled about that but where is Miss Kitty? Didn't she see the squirrel run out? I think she is having fun just playing by herself under there.

"Miss Kitty, the squirrel is gone, get out here now."

Meow.

Oh no, look at her. She is covered in grease. How in the world am I going to get all that grease off her? I can't even tell what color she is under all the grease. This is why I keep baby wipes on the truck. Looks like I have my work cut out for me this time.

It took an entire package of baby wipes and I still didn't get all the grease off her. It's also on the floor, on her seat, in my bed and now all over me too. I should have named her Little Miss Brat Cat. I'm going to have to find a good degreaser to get all this out. What a mess.

Miss Kitty looks very pleased with herself. I, on the other hand, am very upset with her. She has earned the title 'Queen of disasters.' I'm going to have to teach her to clean up her own messes, this is too much work for me. I wonder if it's possible to teach a cat to clean things. It's not like she can hold a broom or even a rag to wipe stuff down. Still, I think there has to be something she could do to help clean up her messes.

Everyone seemed to enjoy the show, they cheered, clapped and I think I heard a few snickers once Miss Kitty finally came out from under the truck. I think I heard a few gasps, probably wondering how I was going to get her cleaned up. This was a little funny, just not to me at that time. I'm glad it put a smile on some of their faces. I probably would have been laughing if it had happened to someone else.

Lord, I know Miss Kitty gets bored sometimes but could you please send her a playmate that won't tear the truck up or make messes or stink or be in the way? Maybe it's better that she just has friends she meets, plays with for a little while and then leaves where they belong. If that is the case then thank you for sending playmates for her but please keep them out of the truck. Thank you, Lord.

Chapter 32

IT'S TIME. READY OR not, I have to go get the tests ran and find out if I have cancer or not. I almost wish they would let me bring Miss Kitty in here with me. It's not like I need someone holding my hand, I just want to know someone is there. She might cause too much of a ruckus if I did bring her so maybe it's best that they don't allow animals in here.

I hope I don't have a heart attack during all these tests. They said to plan on being here at least three hours or more. Just how many tests do they need to run? If they need to check my pulse, they might decide they have to admit me, I know it's racing. Breathe, deep breaths, let out slowly, now walk in the door. Everything is going to be fine; it's just testing today. Stay calm.

Blood, urine, cat scan, you name it. It took at little over four hours. The consultation with Doctor Kutz was regarding chemo and radiation treatments. It was overwhelming and I can't think straight. This just isn't real. It's all just a nightmare and I'm going to wake up some place and laugh about it. Only, it's not funny and I'm not asleep. No more pretending it's not happening. I need to think. I need to plan. I hear my heartbeat in my ears and that's about all I can hear. What is going to happen to Miss Kitty?

I am going to wait for the test results before I notify the family, there is no need to get them all worried if they are negative. How am I going to tell the kids? The grandkids? Who do I ask to take Miss Kitty? I need distance from here. I need to get back to work. There isn't anything I can do about anything at the moment.

Dispatch seems a little worried about sending me back out on the road right now. They don't want me to be too distracted to drive. Do they see the panic or terror in my eyes? I see their point but I can't sit around just waiting. I need to be doing something. They are looking for a load, even if they don't think it's such a good idea. I want a long run, one that goes far, far away.

Atlanta. That's where the load goes. At least I will be so focused on all the traffic there I can forget about my troubles here. Miss Kitty is ready to get back on the road. This is the best thing I know of that we can do, just keep working. I don't feel sick or weak, there is no reason I can't continue to work.

***

"Ugh, I can't breathe. What are you doing Miss Kitty?" She is laying on my neck purring and her hair is getting in my mouth ad nose. Can she sense there is something wrong?

"You need to get out of my face." I keep trying to push her away but she keeps coming back trying to get right in my face and snuggle against me. What is her problem?

"Let me up, we need to get up and get rolling. Get up and let me up, I have to make the coffee."

She didn't want to get off me this morning. The coffee is going and we are doing our pretrip, Miss Kitty is staying right by my side and even tripping me every now and then. She is crowding me and making it hard to get anything done. She definitely knows something is wrong. Is she scared too? It will most definitely have a huge impact on her life. Cats can sense emotion; does she understand any of what is going on? I'm a jumble of emotion, it must be very confusing to her.

***

Big trucks should not be allowed in the middle of Atlanta. I know trucks are supposed to stay on the loop around Atlanta but sometimes you have to make a delivery inside the loop. I've been inside the loop a few times but never in as far as the aquarium. This is insane how they expect a big truck to get in down here.

The dock is at an angle and inside the building. Talk about backing blind. I have to get out every few feet to make sure I'm not hitting anything inside because I can't see my trailer at all. I can't see the dock. I can't see the support pillars I have to squeeze between. A road crew working nearby came to inform me that if I hit the curb or jumped it I would get a hefty fine. Now they are watching me. You think they would at least try to hold back the traffic for me. Nope, they just stand there watching me. No one has offered to help spot me or anything. They are putting my skills to the test today. Let's hope I don't fail; it could bring down the whole building. Wouldn't that be fun. Not.

It took me almost 45 minutes to get in here. I would have been in a lot sooner if I hadn't had to keep stopping for traffic to get around me. No one would help stop the traffic for me to get lined up and in the dock. I asked someone how other drivers do this and they said this was the first time they had seen a truck as big as mine get in here so they didn't know how to help. Wonderful, just wonderful. I hope I can get back out of here with no issues.

It looks like we get a long run afterall. Florida to Washington. A little over 3,000 miles. That is a good load. I will dead-head down to Florida to pick it up. That just means I drive down with an empty trailer to get the load. I get paid all miles, loaded or empty so it's all the same to me. There are still quite a few companies who only pay their driver the loaded miles. They can really take advantage of a driver that way. I'm glad I have a good company to work for.

***

The docks here are what we call open air docks. We back up to a platform outside of the warehouse and they load us from there. We have to do a walk-through inspection before loading so I'm back here in the trailer making sure everything is clean before they come out to inspect.

"Miss Kitty? What are you doing back here? How did you get out of the truck? Let's get you back inside right now before someone notices. They might reject the trailer and refuse to load us. What were you thinking? How did you get up in here?"

Meow.

She must have gotten out at the same time as I did and followed me. I can't believe I didn't see her. She is getting so protective of me.

"You can't be in here while they load it and what if you got locked in? You wouldn't survive back here all the way up to Washington."

Meow.

Lord, please, please don't let anyone see her in here. Just let me get her back into the truck.

Whew, thank you, Lord, for letting me get her back inside the truck before anyone saw her. I don't want kicked out of here or off this load. I really need this run.

"I have to go back out there for the inspection, you stay inside the truck, are we clear? Thank you."

I think she is worried something will happen to me when I leave the truck like maybe I won't come back. She doesn't like me out of her site. How do I assure her I'm going to be just fine?

Lord, thank you for watching out for us in even the smallest of ways. Let Miss Kitty feel your peace as well. Let her know that you will keep both of us safe. Thank you, Lord.

Chapter 33

"RAIN, RAIN GO AWAY. *Come back another day.*" It has been raining for days, it never seems to stop. I didn't expect it to rain the entire trip when I asked for a long run. This is bringing my mood down and getting depressing. A little rain is fine, everything looks so bright and clean afterwards but day after day of nothing but dark clouds and rain makes me want to stay in bed and hide all day.

Miss Kitty hates the rain. It echoes through the truck when it hits and I think she feels under attach because she hides all day and lays across my neck all night. She doesn't even get out to do the pretrips with me. Her favorite hiding spot is behind the cat box and under the glove box in the footwell area. She feels safe there.

***

Nothing looks pretty or special, we don't get out much to even stretch our legs and it makes the trip feel twice as long. Dreary. That's the way to describe how it looks and how it makes us feel. We saw a glimpse of sunshine a couple of times but it was short-lived and not enough to brighten our mood.

We finally made it to Washington. It's still raining. Shouldn't the earth be flooded by now?

I received the dreaded call from the doctor this morning. Not good. He wants me back as soon as possible to do surgery. It is for sure cancerous. It needs removed as soon as possible. They want me to do radiation even if

I don't do chemo. I don't want to. I changed my mind; I don't want to do this anymore. I'm beyond scared, I'm terrified.

Doctor Kutz said I have a cycle cell anemia which is a disease that creates crescent shaped blood cells. They snag on things and can group together and form clots. They think that is how this started out, a clot formed from those cells and the cancer formed in the clot. It is located inside the salivatory gland on the right side and to remove it they have to take the salivatory gland and two inches of surrounding tissue. There is a very high possibility of paralysis due to all the tendons and ligaments in that area of the neck. Even after they remove it, providing they get it all, the likely hood of it returning is extremely high. They said five years is the most I can hope for it to remain dormant.

Dispatch said they can get me a load back to Dallas and I can deadhead back to the yard from there. They know the urgency of getting this taken care of as fast as possible. I, on the other hand, want to put it off as long as possible. I know I can't do that; it will just grow and get worse and then it won't be a simple surgery.

It's time I make the calls to everyone, let them know what is going on and see who will take Miss Kitty. I need to figure out where to stay, I live in the truck but I can't stay in the truck while I'm going through all the treatments. How am I going to survive without working? I don't have the money to take off work for months to do the treatments. I have a lot to think about and do before we get back to Texarkana.

***

The calls were unsettling, everyone was shocked. I still haven't figured out who is going to take Miss Kitty yet. My friend Sasha said she would watch Miss Kitty while I have the surgery. She is coming to the yard to help me for a few days. I still don't have a place to stay for all the treatments. They said it would take about 6 weeks for the initial treatments then we would re-evaluate and see what should happen next. I need to have someone with me because I'll be too sick to take care of myself the majority of the time. There will be times I won't even be able to get out of bed by myself.

I really don't want to do this; I'm scared I might not make it through this. What if something goes wrong? We just got back to Texarkana and I'm afraid to get out of the truck. They tell me the worst that could happen is a little paralysis. They are so wrong; my nerves are what's going to do me in. I'm going in to do all the pre-op tests and what not then tomorrow they will do the surgery. Lord, help me.

***

I'm at the hospital but I can't bring myself to walk inside. Is this really the right thing? If I have enough faith, I should be able to ask God for healing. I'm afraid I might lack the faith for that. Please forgive me Lord, I know you are a God of healing and you can give me a miracle but I also know you have given doctors a gift. Is this lack of faith or is it trusting that God has given the doctor a gift and I have been led to follow that path? Here I go, we did all the pre-op stuff and it's time for the surgery. Is it too late to back out? If I go through the doors, I'm committed to it but if I stay out here, I can go back to the truck and hit the road. I'm going in, may God's will be done, I am ready.

Lord, give me peace and keep me calm through this. Be with me and keep me safe. Watch over Miss Kitty while I'm away.

OK, here I go, I can do this.

***

I'm drowsy but I'm awake. My son, his wife and kids came all the way from Colorado to be with me but they aren't able to stay. I can't remember our visit very well because of the medicine I had to take but it was a wonderful surprise and I love them so very much. It meant the world to me that they came all the way down here for me. They were afraid that this might be the last time they would have to see me and wanted to be able to say goodbye if the worst happened. Thank goodness it didn't.

Doctor Kutz wants me to stay in here long enough to check that I don't have any problems or complications then I get to leave. He said it looks like they got it all and everything looks good. I have a little bit of paralysis but he said it should go away or at least get better with time.

It's done and over with and I'm still alive. Thank you, Lord. No matter how scared I was, I knew God would see me through or I would be joining him in heaven. Why feel fear when it's a winning outcome either way. That's human emotion for sure, God gives peace and not fear. He plainly tells us not to worry but we are human and that is what we do best. Forgive me, Lord.

It's time to get back to the truck, I can't wait to see Miss Kitty, I know she misses me and I really need to see her. I haven't found anyone to take care of her so I could go through the treatments. I have decided I'm not going to do them; I honestly don't know how I could. There really isn't anything it will accomplish. They said it was still going to come back whether I have the treatments or not. I can't afford to take that kind of time off if it's not going to make a difference.

***

"Where is Miss Kitty?"

My friend Sasha was supposed to watch her while I was in the hospital but I when I got back to the truck, she was nowhere to be found. Why isn't she in the truck?

"I went in the truck to feed her but she didn't want me in there and she jumped out. She was looking all around the truck and then just took off. I couldn't find her to get her back in."

"What? How long has she been missing? Have you looked for her? Where is she?"

"She is around here somewhere; I've seen her by the truck a couple times but she runs off when I get close. She won't come when I call her but she has been staying close to the truck."

"Miss Kitty! Little Miss Kitty! Where are you?"

"Look, there she comes, she was just waiting for you to come back. I told you she was here." Sasha sounds relieved to see her.

"There you are, have you been out searching for me? I made sure someone would be here to take care of you, why didn't you stay in the truck?"

Meow.

"See, she is fine. I don't think she liked me smelling like Poochie and she obviously didn't want me in her truck."

"Are you still holding a grudge against her for bringing Poochie in your truck?"

Meow.

"Thanks for keeping an eye on her and making sure she had food and water, even if it wasn't in the truck." I'm so thankful it didn't get too cold for her to be outside. She can be quite a little brat cat.

***

Dispatch gave me the entire week off and I plan on taking advantage of every minute of it. I feel like Frankenstein's monster with all the stiches across my neck. It looks like I had my throat cut. I guess I did.

I can't take any of the pain killers on the truck so before I can head out again, I have to turn in all the pain killers to dispatch so they can be assured I won't get caught with them on the road. That could cost me my cdl. I wouldn't do that; I can handle a little pain.

***

I called Doctor Kutz to see when he wanted me in for a follow up appointment but he said since I wasn't going to follow his instructions on the chemo or radiation there was no need for a follow up appointment. The nurse could remove the tube and the stitches but I needed to find another doctor if I need anything else. I sure know how to lose a doctor.

Lord, thank you for seeing me through the surgery and keeping me safe. Thank you for watching over Miss Kitty while she was out looking for me. Give the kids' safe travel back to Colorado and keep everyone safe out on the road. Thank you, Lord.

***

I was able to get the drain tube and the stitches out by the nurse this morning, everything looks good so they gave me the release to go back to work. My first load is a short one, dispatch is not very convinced I should get too far away, just in case. That's fine. I have plenty of extra time on the load so I can rest if need be. I do believe they are worried about me. That actually makes me feel better, knowing they care.

Thank you, Lord for getting me through this. Thank you for being there with me. Thank for all you have done for me and all you are still doing for me. Thank you, Lord.

Chapter 34

I FEEL A LITTLE weak sometimes and tire rather quickly but I'm doing fine. I had to make Miss Kitty stay off my neck. She wasn't very happy about that. She still sticks right by me and gets under my feet occasionally but she is starting to relax a little, now that the worst is over.

It's been five months since the surgery. I know I might have to go through this again in five years but I can't worry about that now. I'm fixed and doing quite well; the paralysis hasn't entirely gone away and I will probably have it for the rest of my life. That's ok, I'm still alive and all is good. Life goes on.

Loads are slowing down and the economy isn't looking good right now. There are a few companies going out of business. I talked to dispatch and they assure me everything is fine and the company won't be shutting down any time soon. I'm hoping that's true; a lot of drivers are out of work right now. I would have never believed this was possible. How are the stores going to stay open if the trucks aren't running and bringing the products in? Then again, what product will they even have to haul if the plants are shutting down?

We had an appointment for five this morning but no one was here. I have tried calling and dispatch has tried getting in touch with the company but no one has responded to either of us. I thought I might be in the wrong place because not only is no one here but there is nothing here. The place looks abandoned. I let Miss Kitty out to play for a while as I walked around searching for any signs someone was here but I couldn't find anyone and neither did Miss Kitty. Dispatch has requested we give them till nine at least to see if anyone shows up.

8:59 am a pickup truck drives by the lot, backs up and turns in. I grab the paperwork in case they work here or can tell me if this is the right location but the guy starts to drive off as I approach. What the heck?

"Hey, excuse me, do you work here?" I yell to get his attention.

He stops and waits for me to get to his window but doesn't roll it down.

"Excuse me sir, do you work here?"

He holds a finger up telling me to wait. I wait. And wait. And wait. Finally, I knock on his window and he looks up and holds his finger up to wait again. I've been waiting for almost 20 minutes, what is this guy's problem? I just need to know if he works here or knows anything about the place.

Finally, he rolls the window down so we can speak but holds his finger up again. How rude. He is writing something down on a clip board so I wait for him to finish.

"We closed this plant down three days ago so I don't understand what you are doing here." He finally says.

"This is where I was told to deliver the product to, did they go out of business?"

"Not entirely but the only plant left open in Alabama is about 200 miles away and I'm trying to figure out why you are here."

"You could have asked, I could have shown you the bill of lading, it gives this address and a brief paragraph of directions on how to get into this facility." I offered him the bills but he waved them away.

"I assumed you had this address or you wouldn't be here. I have been calling trying to figure out who ordered something shipped to this plant. Like I said, we closed this plant 3 days ago. We gave all our suppliers notice weeks ago. If I hadn't been going up to check one of the buildings up the hill, no one would have known you were here."

"I have been calling all the numbers I was given and dispatch has been trying to find out what is going on as well. So, am I supposed to go to the other plant? Is that where they want this load?"

"No, that's the problem, we no longer need the product you would be delivering to this plant." I offered him the bills again just in case he needed to verify the product but he waved them away again.

Miss Kitty decides she needs to come check out what's going on. She sniffs the vehicle and jumps on his hood to get a better look at him.

"Miss Kitty, don't be rude, he doesn't want you on his truck staring at him."

I grab her off the truck and hold onto her so he doesn't think she is a stray running around.

"I'm sorry, this is Miss Kitty and she is just curious, we have been waiting here since five this morning and you are the first person she has seen here. She just wants to introduce herself I guess."

"There are wild animals out here that might want to make a meal of her, you might want to keep her in the truck for her own safety."

"Thank you. Have you found out where I am supposed to deliver this load? I don't want to sit here if this isn't even the right location."

"Not yet, if you can wait a little longer, I should have some answers. I'll come back and let you know."

"You're leaving? How long do you think it will take to find out where the load needs to be? If the only other plant here in Alabama doesn't want the load, then I should be heading to where ever the load needs to be."

"That's the problem, I don't know and can't tell you anything at this time. Just sit back and relax until I can get you headed in the right direction."

"Alright, thank you sir. Um, what was your name?"

He rolled his window up and drove off leaving us standing there not knowing what to do. I contacted dispatch again but they don't have any answers either. So, we wait.

I have sent messages and called a few times throughout the day, no one knows anything and dispatch has requested I wait for the gentleman to return. Dispatch called him a gentleman, not me, I have a few other things I would like to call him right about now. I have waited all day and now the sun is going down. He has not returned and dispatch knows nothing. They were a little upset I didn't even find out the guy's name but I told them he just rolled the window up and drove off. What, was I supposed to try to chase him down?

***

The sun came up and we still don't know a thing. I'm standing out here drinking my coffee watching Miss Kitty play. I have no idea just how long we will be sitting here waiting. On the bright side, it was a beautiful sunrise.

About nine, the guy drove up and rolled down his window. He doesn't look like he has any answers yet. Sigh. I better go talk to him. He is the only contact I have with the customer. Be nice, Do Not Be Rude. I have to remind myself that customer service is my job.

"Good morning, good news, I hope. Have they told you where I need to go this lovely morning?"

"*No, they have a plant up in New York that might accept it. There is a plant in Memphis I'm waiting to hear back from, they might possibly use the product on your truck. I just came to check if you were still here so I know how to get in touch with you as soon as I do find out.*" This is his update for me, no answers yet. Just wonderful.

"I'm still here. I can give you my contact information if you would like."

"*No, I'll just come back when I know something.*"

"Can I at least get your contact information?"

"*I'm Dan, I'll be back when I know something.*" He gave his name finally, that's something.

He rolled his window up and drove off again. That was not contact information. All I got was a first name and no way to contact him what so ever. This is just wonderful. Dispatch says the best thing to do is just wait patiently for him to return because they don't have any other options available either. Great, let's wait on Dan.

It's eleven and Dan is just returning. If he doesn't have any news this time, I'm asking dispatch if I can drop the load at a drop yard so I can keep rolling. When they finally figure it out, they can send a driver to deliver it. I will be far away from here.

"*I have good news, the plant in Memphis will accept the load. Here is their address. Good luck.*"

I take the paper he handed me but as soon as it leaves his hand, he rolled his window up and drove off leaving me standing there, again, with a ton of questions and no one to ask. What a gentleman indeed.

I have informed dispatch and they agreed I had best get up to that plant as quickly as possible before they change their minds even though they have not been able to confirm anything at this time. They wished me luck as well.

***

I pull up to the gate after five knowing it might be too late to get in but I have to try. I got here as quickly as I could, they can't blame me for this whole debacle.

"Hi, I have a load that was supposed to be delivered at the plant in Alabama but they rerouted me to your plant. I don't have an appointment but can you check to see if they will receive it?"

"Sure, I can check for you. Wait, do you have a cat in there?"

"Yes sir, this is Miss Kitty."

"We don't allow pets of any kind in here. I can check on the load but you will have to park off the property. I'll send someone out to you."

"Just where off property are you wanting me to park in order for them to be able to find me?"

"Go back down to the road and take the other drive way. It leads to that other warehouse over there." He points. "They leave at five so you shouldn't have any problems getting in and turning around then you can park in their drive facing us. I'll send someone over as soon as I have any information."

"Ok, thank you."

This keeps getting better and better. I did as requested and now I'm waiting again. I hope they figure this out, I'm sick and tired of this load. Texarkana isn't too far away, maybe I can take it to the yard and let them worry about it.

***

Knock, knock.

"Yes? Are you here to let me know what to do about the load?"

"Yes ma'am, I need you to drop it right here so I can take it in to get unloaded. I'll bring the trailer back out as soon as they are finished."

"Thank you so much. I'll unhook right now. It is ok for me to stay parked here, isn't it?"

"Yes ma'am, this is where they have all the drivers who can't come into the yard park. I assume you have a pet on the truck?"

Of course, Miss Kitty pops up to greet him the minute he refers to her.

"Oh, you have a cat. No wonder they didn't let you through the gate."

"This is Miss Kitty. She wants to sniff you to see if you are a good person, is that alright?"

"Oh, sure, I love cats." He says with a big smile.

Miss Kitty was satisfied so I got out and dropped the trailer. Now we wait again. Joy, joy.

Since we didn't know if they would accept the load or when I might get empty, dispatch hasn't had a chance to find another load for us. This would be the ideal time to request a load to Colorado to see the family. A little guilt about how I've had to sit for so long on this load might help to find that load for me.

I put in the request and they found a load right away. We got a load from Memphis to Denver loading first thing in the morning. I didn't even have to say anything about how long I had to wait with this load. Good deal, we need some time to visit, I haven't been through in a while.

Lord, thank you for giving us the opportunity to go home for a little while, we need a break. Thank you for keeping us safe and thank you for this load finally getting delivered.

Chapter 35

I THINK MISS KITTY recognizes the smell of home. She is standing at the window waiting for me to roll it down even though she knows I won't until we are completely stopped. She usually stays in her seat waiting patiently but I think she is excited about being back and seeing everyone.

The plan was to stay at my son's house this visit but of course Miss Kitty tried to take over the house like she did at Babygirl's house. She wanted nothing to do with their kitties and made that known often and loudly. She chased them into the bedrooms and guarded the doors so they couldn't come out. The kids had to carry their kitties out of the rooms to the food dishes before they could put them down to eat and stand right there with them or Miss Kitty would chase them back to the bedrooms. They had to move the litter boxes into the bedrooms because Miss Kitty wouldn't even let them out to go potty. The kids were so scared of Miss Kitty guarding the doors, they too were afraid to come out even to go to the bathroom. They changed their mind about wanting Miss Kitty there all night so I have to take her back to the truck and we sleep there.

Everyone gets together for picnic lunches then we gather at my son's house for BBQ dinners and games. The adults watch movies together after the kids go to bed and Miss Kitty guards the bedroom doors. Babygirl lets two of her kids stay over and wakes up the other two to take home then switch the next night. She drops me and Miss Kitty off at the truck on her way home then someone picks us up in the morning and we do it all over again. I wish we could be here more often; we could all do things together on a regular basis. Wouldn't that be great?

I tried to leave Miss Kitty with my daughter once, to give my son a break, while I went shopping for supplies but Babygirl said she stayed at the window looking out waiting for me the whole time. She didn't let anyone touch her and she wouldn't even play with the kids. She hissed at her cats and just watched for me at the window until I got back. She said it was so sad it almost made her cry. Now I can't bring myself to leave her there unless I'm there with her. Miss Kitty seems content as long as I am there with her.

I didn't want this to end. We were able to stay four glorious days before dispatch called me back to work. They had a driver break down about 35 miles away from where I'm at and needed the load rescued. I am the only driver in Colorado at this time so I am the one who has to rescue it.

***

When we got to the other truck, they had a tow truck pulling his tractor out from the trailer. Good thing they have a Freightliner shop right here in town. They have a Peterbilt here too, that's where I take my truck when it needs fixed. I got out to get the bills and ask him if he wanted the empty trailer left here at the truck stop or taken to the shop he was going to. He just wants it left here. Miss Kitty followed me to say hi.

"Miss Kitty, what are you doing?"

She jumped up in his truck to see what the problem was, I guess. Or maybe visit the mechanics.

"Miss Kitty, get out of there, the tow truck needs to take that truck into the shop."

He had opened the door to get the bills and I guess Miss Kitty took that as an invitation.

"Miss Kitty, get out of there. You can't fix the truck; it needs to go to the shop."

"*That's quite the cat you have there. She seems to like being in a truck. She jumped right up there like she belongs there. I have thought about bringing my cat out here with me but I didn't think a cat would take to the truck so I never* tried. I think I'll see what mine thinks once I get the truck fixed and back on the road. Do you have any problems with keeping her in the truck that I should be aware of? Do I need to train her?"

"Not really, Miss Kitty usually stays right with me or right by the truck. She does like to check out other trucks every now and then, like she is looking for a better house. I don't know of any special training, just keep her inside for about a month before trying to let her out. That's just for her to get used to that being her new home. It would be best if she was trained to walk on the leash. Miss Kitty does have to be on the leash sometimes but she hates it."

"That's good to know. I think I'll swing by and pick my cat up to see how she does. Thanks."

Miss Kitty jumps out and back into her own truck which made the other driver laugh. We both agreed that his truck was not acceptable to her standards. I hope his kitty likes his truck, I think having a cat on the truck is great, I couldn't imagine not having one anymore.

Miss Kitty watched as the tow truck took the other truck away, I wonder what she is thinking. Was she disappointed there wasn't a mechanic in that truck? She loves mechanics. It would be nice to know what she thinks about things, she is so curious and wants to know everything that goes on around her.

"Maybe next time we see that driver he will have his kitty with him. Do you want to see kitties in other trucks?"

Meow.

"That didn't sound like a yes but I'm going to pretend it did. You need to get along with other pets. I'm not talking about the critters you try to bring on the truck, I'm talking about the pets' other drivers keep on their trucks."

Meow.

Driving back and forth across the country can be rather boring when you don't have someone to share it with. Thank you, Lord, for sending Miss Kitty to me. Thank you for giving me the best of the best truck kitty ever.

***

Wow, this is a beautiful sunset here in Kansas. It stretches across the sky turning all kinds of oranges, pinks and reds. The sky is filled with color. There has to be a dozen colors blending without clashing. That is true beauty. We should be up in time to see the sunrise in the morning as well. Nothing to obstruct the view out here, we are so fortunate to enjoy this as part of our day.

Thank you, Lord, for the beauty you have given us. This has been the perfect ending to our day and proof of your love and thoughtfulness. A little reminder that you are always here and always watching out for us. I love you so much Lord.

Chapter 36

I was called in to the yard by dispatch today. I was delivering my load in Houston so I was close enough not to need a load to get back to the yard. I'm just deadheading up there to find out what this is all about. I don't think I have done anything wrong. We have been on time for all our pick-ups and deliveries and as far as I know, no one has had any complaints against us. They wouldn't tell me what it's about, they just said they would be waiting for me, they have a matter they need to discuss with me.

***

As I pull up to the gate, I notice something is very wrong. The main building looks dark and there are very few cars here. It looks like the only cars are in the drivers parking lot. What in the world is going on here? Did they have something happen inside the building today? Did they have to evacuate for some reason? Why does it look empty?

"Good morning, are you bringing the truck back?" Asks a smiling guard. It must not be too bad if the guard is smiling. I guess I'm just letting my unease get the best of me.

"Good morning, I'm just here to speak with dispatch. They called me in to talk to me about something important I think." Wait, did he just ask if I was bringing my truck back like turning it in? Why would he ask a question like that? Something is wrong. I can feel it.

"Oh, well you missed them. Everyone has already left." He said, still smiling.

"What? They know I'm on my way in, they are the ones who requested me to be here. Why would they leave? Did something happen here today? It's too early for everyone to leave for the day."

"They didn't tell you? I'm so sorry, there is no one working in the terminal at all. The big wigs came in at eight this morning and told everyone to clear their desks out, they were shutting down." Why is he still smiling. He is really creeping me out.

"What? What do you mean shutting down? They can't shut down; they didn't even give us notice of their intent. They can't shut down just like that." I snap my fingers.

"They can and they did. They didn't give anyone notice until eight this morning. No one is working except the shop and those of us here at the guard gate. That's all the people needed just to receive the trucks as they are brought back in." Why is he still smiling?

"This isn't possible. Where are the drivers supposed to go? They can't just throw us out with nothing."

"I don't know what to tell you, I was just told to check the trucks in and let the drivers get their things cleaned out. We aren't to allow them to take the trucks out of the yard. That's all the instructions we were given and to keep a smile on our face so the drivers didn't get violent." That explains the smile. They must be paying the guards hazard pay to deal with a bunch of angry drivers. Not something I would want to do for sure.

"Well, this is my truck, I'm buying it and I shouldn't have to clean it out, I'm planning on keeping it. I haven't even had the opportunity to look for another company to work for. Are they expecting me to clean out my truck and turn it in as well? I won't abandon my truck until I find out what's going on. Can stay here for now until I get this straightened out?"

"I don't have any answers for you, I'm sorry. I don't know if they will allow you to stay on the property or not but I won't kick you out while I'm working as long as you aren't causing any problems while you are here but I can't allow you to leave with the truck. We have been told to call the sheriff if anyone tries to take the trucks out of the gate."

"Thanks, I won't be causing problems but I will be making a lot of calls and I don't plan on leaving until I have some answers. Thank you."

I can't believe it, no warning or anything. I tried calling dispatch but no one is answering the phones. I have tried calling every contact I have for this company but haven't been able to reach even one person. Is this our Christmas bonus? This is one heck of a way to end the year. New year, new job. I need to know what is happening with my truck. I better call and warn Sasha, she might not know about this and I don't want her stranded out there on the road if they take the truck away.

"Hey, how far away from the yard are you?"

"*I'm in Chicago, why?*" She doesn't sound upset, I better break the news hard and fast.

"They just shut down the company, you might want to get back here asap and clean your truck out."

"*What? They can't do that to us! No way, someone is lying to you.*" She can deadhead down here before they can stop her and leave her stranded out on the road.

"I'm here at the yard right now. No one is here except the guard and the guys at the shop. The main building is dark and no one is answering the phones. I tried the doors and they're all locked. I'm not kidding, you need to get back here asap. Don't mess around, they might come after your truck."

"*What? No way. I have to make some calls. I'll talk to you later.*"

Click.

That went better than I expected, I thought she would start yelling at me. I guess they didn't tell any of the other drivers anything either. They should have at least sent out a message to all the drivers so we could at least have the chance to find a new job. There are over a thousand drivers that work here and around a hundred and fifty of us are buying our trucks, what are we supposed to do? We have a contract with the financing company, this company and the brokers. I guess I better start making a few calls myself and see if I can find out if I can take my truck to another company pronto because I have nowhere to go. My contract with the finance company lists this company as the lien holder so I don't know if I can even drive my truck off the yard without being arrested for theft.

Good news is that every company I have called is more than willing to hire me. Bad news is I can't take my truck, it's tied up in contracts with this company and I have to surrender it. I lost all the money I have invested in it as well as my escrow and maintenance accounts. Now, I have to choose which company to work for and decide whether I want to be a company driver or try a lease purchase program. I called about eight companies that I am familiar with. They were as shocked as I was that my company had shut down. I have a little time to figure out which one to work for while I get the truck cleaned out.

***

I have too much stuff. I hope they let me stay all night here, there is no way I can get everything packed up and into the car in just a couple hours' time. A few more trucks have come in and I have heard a lot of yelling. I feel sorry for the guards at the gate, they didn't have anything to do with this and since the drivers weren't notified on what was happening, the guards have to be the ones to tell the drivers and take the brunt of their anger. Who else are the drivers going to yell at? There isn't anyone else here. I noticed they have two guards instead of just one at the gate now. They might need more than that pretty soon.

Lord, please let me choose the right company to work for. I have been with this company so long; I don't know where to go.

***

Miss Kitty is freaking out. She can not understand what is happening. She is meowing and jumping around the truck so much she is constantly getting in my way. I'm going to have to put her in the carrier and leave her in the car until I finish getting everything out of the truck. She is not happy at all.

I decided to go work for another company who does the exact same loads as this one did. It won't be so hard to adjust since they have the same customers and everything. I hope this is the right decision. They don't have Peterbilt trucks so I'm going to see how well I like Kenworth. They should be very similar; they merged the companies not too long ago. The body style is different and I'm guessing the interior is too. I haven't been in a Kenworth for over 15 years, I wonder if I will like them better than I did back then? I sure hope so.

***

I decided to try their lease purchase program and I'm getting a silver truck. I hope I don't forget and lose the truck in a truck stop. That would be quite embarrassing to say the least. We have to stay at a motel while I go through orientation, I hope Miss Kitty likes the motel, she will have to stay in there by herself during the day while I'm in the classroom.

My friend Sasha was able to go back to the company she first started driving with so she won't be coming to work over here with me. I don't know if we will still get the opportunity to run into each other on the road like we used to but who knows, we are both still driving all over the country even if it's not for the same company anymore.

I have to sign all the contracts for the lease purchase deal they have. I almost had my other truck paid off when I lost it and I'm not sure I want to do this type of deal. Lord, don't let this be a big mistake.

The truck payments are going to be quite a bit higher here but it doesn't look like I get the truck paid off any faster than my other truck. I wasn't doing lease purchase; I was just purchasing it through a finance company last time. I have heard that lease purchase deals are pretty bad with some companies, I hope this isn't one of them. Lord, help me to be making the right decision.

Thank you, Lord, for letting me find a company right away. Thank you for letting me find one who allows Miss Kitty in the truck with me. Thank you that I can be in Tulsa where my cousin lives so I have someone I can visit and stay with if the need arises. Help me not to be taken advantage of in this Lease Purchase deal. Thank you for all you do for me, Lord.

Chapter 37

MISS KITTY SEEMS TO like the motel, she is loving the slick floors. She runs after her fluffy balls and slides over them. Then she gets them and brings them back to me to throw for her and slides over them again. She loves it and is having so much fun. She has been running and sliding around the corner to the bathroom until I heard her hit the toilet pretty hard then she came back in and laid down to rest, I hope she didn't hurt herself.

The first day of orientation went well, not. I almost left. Just walked away and been done with them. Maybe I should have. They are asking something I cannot and will not do. They said Miss Kitty had to be declawed to be on the truck. Don't they know that is abuse? They cut their fingers off at the knuckle and the poor kitty can't hardly walk till it's healed and sometimes not even then if they did it wrong. They can't scratch the truck up, sure, but they can't hardly scratch in the litter box to cover their poop either. It's very painful and causes trust issues they might never get over. That is mutilation and there is no way I'm going to do that to Miss Kitty. I can't believe they require that. I had to pay an extra pet deposit, double what they normally charge but there was no way I would mutilate my baby like that.

If they hadn't backed down from that, I would have left for sure. They do things a little different here and I'm not sure I like it but I should be able to adjust with little to no problems. The fuel card is different and so is the fuel network on where we are allowed to fuel. There are some differences on how they run things as well but I think I will do just fine here.

***

"Miss Kitty, what are you doing? Get back here and leave the food alone. Miss Kitty."

I saw a kitty behind the motel this evening and decided to feed it, it looked hungry and we have plenty of cat food to spare. Miss Kitty did not want to share, she ran out and chased the other little kitty off and ate all the food so it didn't get any.

"Miss Kitty, move out of the doorway, I need to close the door. What is wrong with you? You already chased the kitty away, get back in here."

Meow.

Nope, she is sitting in the door, watching the spot where that other kitty was earlier and she won't move. At all. She won't let me close the door and won't come in or go out. I admit, I did try taking more food out for the other kitty just in case it came back but she ran out there and ate all the food before the other kitty could. It hasn't been back since but she won't move.

"Enough already, get in here so I can close the door." I have to actually move her to get the door closed.

Meowol, meow, meorl.

"You can't be greedy Miss Kitty; you have plenty of food to share. I wasn't trying to keep the kitty, just give it a little food. It looked hungry; you would want someone to give you food if you were hungry."

Growl.

"Miss Kitty, quit being like that."

Growl.

"Fine, you don't like to share, I get that but I do. You are going to have to accept the fact that I might give something to another kitty. It doesn't mean I don't love you or that I want to keep the other kitty, it just means I want to be nice. Deal with it."

Meowol.

"I understand, you are jealous. Work on that because I will give what I want to who I want and as long as you have enough what does it matter?"

Meow.

"No talking back to me. Enough is enough young lady, you need to learn to share. That's all there is to it."

Meow.

She has seen me give food to other animals, not just kitties, some doggies too, so I don't know why she is throwing such a fit this time. I guess she didn't realize it was her food I was giving away before. I hope she doesn't try to get out and chase the other kitty when the maid comes to check the room tomorrow. I might have to ask them not to open the door if I'm not here. I'm sure they have to do that with some of the dogs that stay here.

***

Orientation is almost done and we get to move into the truck this afternoon. I think Miss Kitty likes the motel; I wonder if she will like being back on the truck again? She might want to live in a house that doesn't move all the time. I think she will be fine; she is an excellent truck kitty.

I was able to take a break and have lunch with my cousin. It has been a while since we sat down and caught up with each other. Her husband died a few years ago and neither one of us has had the time to really visit since. She has a rather hectic life and I only have a few minutes as I'm passing through. Maybe with me working for this company I can get through more often and have to time to visit more.

I think I need to get rid of some stuff, this is way too much to fit in the truck. How did it all fit in the other truck? This could take a week to get organized. I might need help. Do I need this much stuff? I have lived on a truck for years and it all seemed so important to have but I don't know when the last time was that I really went through all the stuff. I am going to take a little extra time to get rid of stuff. I'll keep it in the car and if I don't need it by the time I get back, I'm getting rid of it. This is too much.

I can't bring the car in the yard to the truck and can't bring the truck out to the car. Thank goodness they are letting me bring the truck to the motel to do the rest of the move in and organization. Miss Kitty has jumped in and out of the truck to check it out a few times but it was a little distressing for her. I had to keep her in the room with the door closed while I finished up and then let her in the truck to find her spots. I put her pillows and beds in a few places but had to move them a couple times until she found the right spot, she wanted her things to be.

It's time for us to get back to work, we had a little break but we can't afford to wait too long. Our first load goes to California of course, where else would we expect to go right off the bat? At least Miss Kitty will enjoy that. I did let dispatch know places I really don't want to be and places I refuse to go so they can try to avoid sending me there if possible.

Lord, be with us as we head out on the road again. Watch over us and keep us safe. Thank you, Lord.

Chapter 38

~~

THIS TRUCK IS ARRANGED a little different and things just aren't where they are supposed to be when I look for them. Miss Kitty seems to feel the same, she jumps around a lot trying to find just the right spot or looking for her toys since I had to put her toybox in a different place on this truck. We are adjusting.

The truck doesn't seem to have much power up these little hills like the Pete but I suppose it does alright. I'll have to see how it does in the mountains, that is the real test. It shifts a bit rough; I might have to get that looked at. I think it's more than just the difference in the truck. It is a used truck and who knows how the last person who had it drove.

We are heading to San Francisco. It is not truck friendly. I swear it gets worse every year. Not that it was good to begin with. It's not like I haven't been there before and we can't be too picky with a company we have just started working for. This is a decent load mile wise, that's what really matters.

***

Not good, as we were coming up out of Albuquerque, it did a very hard shift, like I almost thought the transmission broke kind of hard. It was a clunk and the truck shuttered really bad, enough to scare Miss Kitty. I'm going to have to call breakdown and tell them about this. I just got the truck and I think it's breaking down.

***

That was useless, they said to keep going, I don't have enough money in my maintenance account to get it fixed yet. I just started working for them, it's my first load, no, I don't have any money in my maintenance account yet. The thing is, this is a newer truck, less than two years old, it should be covered under warrantee. I'm not sure what I think about these guys now. I'll keep going but I don't plan on being broke down along the road and have to get a tow truck. That would cost a lot more than getting it fixed now would. I'm the one who has to pay for it, I'm the one who should make the decision.

It made it to California, I don't know what to think, is it going to be ok? Is it going to leave me stranded somewhere? I guess I'll find out soon enough.

We stopped at a rest area for a little break before going in to the receiver so I could make some calls and let Miss Kitty stretch her legs so she wouldn't want out on the customers property. I got out while I was on the phone so I didn't notice what Miss Kitty was up to. That was a mistake. I knew there was a little pond or whatever but I didn't think Miss Kitty would go to the water so I didn't notice the ducks.

I had just hung up the phone and turned back to the truck when I saw a little duck by the door of the truck and Miss Kitty trying her best to shoo it inside. It couldn't figure out how to get up the steps or it would have. She was right behind it and every time it tried to turn to run away, she would block it so all it could do is try to fly up into the truck. I guess it couldn't figure out how to fly away from the truck or maybe it really was trying to fly inside. In any case, it would try to fly up but land back down and Miss Kitty would block it from leaving and advance until it tried to fly up into the truck again and she would just watch and wait.

I stood there stunned and a little fascinated by what she was doing before I came to my senses and had to put an end to her little game.

"Miss Kitty, you cannot have a duck on the truck. Let it go back to its home and leave it alone."

Mew.

"Miss Kitty, let it go back where it belongs. We talked about what was acceptable pets, ducks are not on the list. Leave it alone."

Mew.

"Young lady, you will listen to me. Leave it alone and get back in the truck, we will discuss this later."

I had to grab her by the neck, shoo the duck away and pull her into the truck with me.

Meow, mew, meow.

"I said a kitty or a puppy dog. Not a duck. Do we need a picture book so you can see what you can and cannot have? There is a reason we can't have other critters on the truck. We have to follow the rules."

Meow.

"It might not seem fair to you but you aren't the one who has to clean up after it or figure out what to feed it. You have to obey my rules and I have to obey the rules for the truck. We are done discussing this. The answer is no." It was pretty cute but no way I'm taking care of a duck on the truck.

Meow.

***

Oh Dear Lord, send your angels to push the truck down. There is a low clearance ahead and no way to slow down enough to stop before we hit it. I can't avoid it so please push the truck down so we don't hit. Thank you, Lord.

Oh my gosh, that was close. There were no warning signs or anything to let us know what was coming up, just the bridge with the clearance printed on it. It had to be God who got us under that bridge. I thought this is the way the directions had us go but I think we might have made a wrong turn somewhere. I'm not sure where we are now. Oh thank goodness, there is the road we need.

This has been quite the ordeal getting here. I don't like the feel of the truck but we made it into the receiver without breaking down and we narrowly avoided a bad situation but God helped us through. We didn't have any problems getting in and getting a door. Miss Kitty seems happy, she has her head out the window smelling the salty, fishy air. She loves that smell, I don't see how, it stinks to me.

Looks like we are getting a load all the way to North Carolina. That's a good run. They should be finished unloading us soon and we will be able to pick it up and head out of California.

"Look Miss Kitty, they have a cat in the truck next to us. OH, they have two. I would get you a kitty friend if you would let it stay in the truck."

Meow.

"You could play while I drive and I could close off the bunk with the curtain so you could play all night up front. Wouldn't that be fun?"

Hiss.

"Really? How do you know you wouldn't like another cat if you don't give it a chance? You kicked the other kitty out before you even got to know her."

Hiss.

"You act like you want a friend when you try to bring all the other critters on the truck, what's wrong with another cat?"

Hiss.

"Fine, no cat. Do you want a doggie on the truck?"

Growl, hiss.

"I take that as a definite no. Alright, no pets, they won't allow anything else. Those are your two choices."

Meow.

"Nope, pick between one of those or nothing at all."

That ended quickly, she jumped down and went in the back. It seems she didn't like her options. Rules are rules. I've seen birds on trucks but there is no way I would even give her that option. I do not want a bird on the truck period. That's not even worth discussing with her. She wants a rat or a mouse or a chicken or a duck or a squirrel but not a cat and especially not a dog. I don't know what to do about her wanting a pet. She can't have what she wants so she will have to be the only pet on the truck. Period.

***

We got all the way out of California before the truck started acting up again. We made it as far as Kingman when the coolant light came on. I checked it first thing this morning and double checked it just now. The coolant is fine. There must be a sensor going out. I'm not sure I like this truck. I'm going to do what they told me to do and keep going till I can't go any further. Let's hope I'm not broke down on the side of the road in the middle of nowhere.

It's getting worse. The light has been on for a while and now it's telling me to shut down or I will cause damage to the engine, what the heck? I have checked the coolant continuously and it's fine. I has to be a sensor. The truck is starting to derate. It keeps dropping the speed down and is telling me it's going to shut off to protect the engine.

I have been able to stop and let it reset then continue driving for a while before it does it again but the almost constant alarm is driving me crazy. Miss Kitty is getting really upset too, she doesn't understand that loud noise and keeps trying to get me to do something about it. What can I do? Just stop and let it reset. That's all I know to do until we can get it fixed.

Lord, thank you for keeping us safe, please keep this truck running and if there is a way to stop the alarm, please let me know. Thank you for getting us in and out of California without any problems.

Chapter 39

BY THE TIME WE reached Oklahoma City, the truck was shutting down all the time. The warnings came on and the engine derated till we were only going 5 mph. I dropped the load at the drop yard in OKC and am heading to Tulsa doing the stop and shut down to reset thing continuously. I have to get the truck fixed at the yard since I still don't have enough money in my maintenance account for repairs.

I am not happy; I lost a load and now I get to sit at the motel again waiting. No clue how long it's going to take, they are checking the transmission and the coolant. At least Miss Kitty liked the idea of coming back to the motel but she tried to go back to the room we had before. I can't believe she remembered which room we stayed in.

***

I have been offered a rental truck but I would have to pay the double pet deposit all over again plus the rental fees as well as the regular truck payment. I think I'll just wait on my truck. Besides, Miss Kitty is having a blast sliding on the floor again. If we ever get our own house, I'm going to make sure we have slick floors for her to slide on. She has her own bed too. She might be getting a little spoiled here.

We've been here four days when they called to say the truck is done. I've spent more time in the motel than I have driving for these guys, I think. Oh well, we have a load here on the yard we can grab and take to Florida. That should be a good run out of here.

Nope, check engine light and coolant light came on just past Memphis. Their advice? Turn the truck off for a little bit and see if it goes away. Of course, it goes away but the question is how long before it comes back on?

All the way down to Alabama we stopped for a bit and continued on, stopped for a little bit and continued on until finally I said I had had enough. We couldn't keep doing this, the alarm will drive us crazy and we will never get the load delivered on time. This is just plain pathetic that they would have their drivers do this.

***

Guess what? We are back in the shop. Do you know that Mobile is actually the birthplace of the Marti-gras? Neither did I until I tried to book a room here. Almost no one has a vacancy and the absolute lowest price I could find anywhere around here was $250 per night. How long is the truck going to be in the shop? Just how much is this going to cost us? Who knows. Just wonderful.

Dear Lord, please help me to stay calm just long enough to get this truck fixed.

We got checked in last night and I didn't ask about coffee, breakfast or anything else so imagine my surprise when I got up this morning and there was no coffee. No coffee in the room, no coffee in the lobby, no coffee anywhere near the motel. For these prices they should have had it waiting the minute I woke up. This just can't be real. No coffee? At a motel that costs $250 per night how can they not have coffee!!

One of the ladies on the housekeeping staff suggested I try sneaking into the motel across the street, they have a full breakfast bar and plenty of coffee. I looked and it was the Hilton. They most definitely will have coffee. Unfortunately, it takes a key card to enter first thing in the morning, I'll have to wait for the lobby to open to get in the door. I went back to my motel to check on Miss Kitty and wait for them to open the lobby but guess what? I locked my key card in the room while I was busy talking to the housekeeper. I need coffee!

No one is at the front desk of this motel till eight, I haven't had coffee and Miss Kitty is upset that she can hear me talking in the hallway but I haven't been in to check on her. This is crazy. I need my coffee or I'm not going to handle this situation well. Please just give me some coffee.

Lord, please help me, I haven't had my coffee and things are going downhill here.

Their suggestion for coffee was to call door dash or grub hub or uber eats. Like I want to pay $12 for a cup of coffee. No thanks. I am checking out. Where am I going to go? Argh! I'll go across the street and give them my sob story and hope they will feel sorry for me and allow me to get a cup of coffee. They actually did me one better, they said they had an early check out and they could get me in a room at the same rate I was paying at the other place as long as I didn't tell anyone.

Guess where I am sitting right now? At the breakfast bar at the Hilton drinking COFFEE. It took me a few trips to grab my things, Miss Kitty and her things but here we are. At the Hilton. Wow, I feel special. I walked into the room and the tv said "Welcome Tory" right on the screen.

The normal rate for this room at this time of the year with Marti-gras going on is over $500 per night. I got a suite. It has a kitchenette, a living room and through the door is the bedroom and bathroom. They put a little magnet outside the door with a paw print letting housekeeping know there is a pet inside. This place is amazing. They have a free wine tasting tonight with sandwiches and fruit and cheese and who knows what but it's free. Miss Kitty can't go, she's not happy about that but no pets are allowed.

There is a huge fireplace right in the middle of the lobby and everything is decorated with lights and beads. They even have a Marti-gras tree that is decorated with beads and Marti-gras trinkets. It's a little fantasy land right here in the hotel. I have to take pictures to send the family, they will never believe me without pictures.

Keep the truck as long as you need, I'm at the Hilton. I didn't actually say that of course but I did call to check on the truck. Still checking it out, no idea when it will be done. Blah blah blah. Whatever. I'm at the

Hilton and they have coffee every single morning ready and waiting for me. I could live here.

***

Six days. That is how long it took to fix the truck this time. I swear if one more thing goes wrong with it I'm giving it back to them. They are trying to sell me a lemon. I can't work like this; I'm paying more in motel fees than I'm making. This isn't working for me. The load was rescued of course and I'm heading to Georgia to pick up a different load.

Half way to the shipper the warning lights are back on. I don't care. I informed dispatch they can either get me a load to the yard or I will bringing whatever load I have to the yard. I am not keeping this truck.

They did get us back to the yard right away, they had us swap a couple times but we made it. I told them I got a lemon and wanted something that actually ran if I was going to stay working for them. Yep, I was upset. I had to do a whole lot of stopping for a bit here and there to let the truck reset in order to make it to the yard and it took forever.

I chose another silver Kenworth and spent two days transferring everything from one truck to the other. That is hard work. I bought a little trailer that I could pull behind my car and put some things in there so I didn't have quite so much stuff to put back in the truck. That is the reason it took so long to make the move. Miss Kitty did not like the move. No motel and just throwing stuff out of one truck and loading it in the other or taking it to the trailer.

Done, we have a truck and now we need a load as soon as we can to get away from here. I'm trying to be calm about things and just get back on the road. A load came in to the yard at two in the morning. I'm taking it.

Chapter 40

"ON THE ROAD AGAIN, *just can't wait to get on the road again.*" I am not a good singer; Miss Kitty growled at me and batted my leg telling me to stop.

The load made it to Phoenix on time, truck ran fine, things are all good now. We are heading to Wisconsin; it's been a while since we have been up there. Maybe we can drive through the Dells, that is so pretty. I want to take some time off up in that area one of these days. Just to relax. Not in winter.

Brrr! It is cold up here. We had a few delays due to accidents on the way up, nothing major but we were running just a little behind. They said bring the load on in as soon as I get here so, here I am but they didn't wait for us. Oh, I'm not that late but the power went off up here and they had to send everyone home. The guard said they left instructions for me to just go right to the docks and park it for the night. Said as soon as the power comes back on in the morning, they will get me unloaded.

I turned the truck off and tried to turn the apu (auxiliary power unit) on but it shows the red triangle. It's not working. I guess I will have to keep the truck running all night, there is no way we are going to freeze to death in the truck. I'll get it looked at later. I hope it doesn't start snowing.

The apu is a little generator that runs heat or ac and an inverter so you can run your appliances in the truck without having to keep the truck running. It uses the fuel from your tanks. It keeps the batteries charged as well.

***

Meow. Scratch, scratch.

"Miss Kitty, you do not need out. It's cold out there and I'm not leaving the door open for you." I saw a critter moving around out there, she probably wanted to check it out but it's too cold to let her out.

Meow. Scratch, scratch.

"Absolutely not, do you understand how cold it is? If I let you out, I'm closing the door behind you."

Meow. Scratch, scratch.

"Fine, but don't ask to get right back in, you can stay out there and freeze."

I give in and open the door. I closed it right after she jumped out to prove my point. She went half way to the parking lot and stopped, turned around like she was coming back then she realized the door was indeed closed. She squatted down and she is staring at me. I am staring back. This is some sort of a standoff, I think.

I wait a good five minutes before I opened the door and she came running back in. She is a half frozen little fluff ball.

Meow, merowl, meow.

"I told you to stay in the truck. Next time you better listen to me."

Meow.

"Yes, I know I closed the door, I didn't want to freeze in the truck."

Meow.

I let her have the last word since I know how insulted she was. She did come and snuggle up to watch tv with me so I would know all was forgiven. She probably wanted to find a bunny to bring on the truck.

***

The power was back on when they came in and we got unloaded right away. We need to get back South or we are going to have to get this apu fixed. It's too cold not to have the heater working and takes too much fuel to keep the truck running all the time. I'm the one who pays for the fuel.

We actually got a load going to Joplin and from there were able to run back by the yard. I was getting ready to write up the apu for repair but there was a repair guy working on the apu on the truck next to us and I got out to ask what I should do to fix mine. He hooked the computer up, changed the fuse and went back to the other truck. He didn't even write it up. No charge, how awesome is that?

Lord, I know that was a blessing from you. Thank you for always watching out for me and taking care of me.

***

This truck seemed to be running great, everything was going great. We have seen a few customers we had with the last company who have recognized Miss Kitty when we pulled in. What's that expression 'Never count your eggs until they hatch'? Well, just when you think everything is going great, something is bound to go wrong. It's some sort of fact of life, I think. Isn't that like a part of Murphy's law?

As we pulled in to fuel, warning lights came on. Great, not again. I came to a stop waiting for the island to clear and couldn't move. Not forward, not backward, nothing. I couldn't pull up to the pump and I couldn't back out so I left the truck blocking the fuel island with my flashers on and went in to talk to the shop. They said they would have to tow it in as soon as the tow truck got back from a service call, I just need to inform the fuel desk and they will have someone put the cones out behind my truck.

I had to call breakdown to inform them of what was going on and knowing I still don't have enough money in my maintenance account, it's in the negative over $6,000 already and that's just from what the shop at the yard charges since that's the only way to charge the repairs. I would have to pay out of my pocket at any other shop. I feared what they would tell me. I never had to worry about stuff like this with the last company, they always extended me credit if my funds ran low because they knew I'd get the money back in the account with just a few runs. They fought for warrantee repairs so I never had to worry about arguing with a mechanic whether it was under warrantee. This company just wants it paid and doesn't care if it comes out of the driver's pocket when it should have been under warrantee.

I'm just sitting here at the fuel island waiting to hear the decision on what is going to happen. Are they going to get the truck fixed or am I going to be stranded at the truck stop until I can figure out how to pay for the repair. I thought this truck was doing so well, what in the world just happened? I don't think it was anything I did; it didn't show any signs of a pre-existing problem. I've been driving it for a while and then all of a sudden, it broke.

Ring, ring.

"Hello."

"*Are you still at the truck stop?*" Dispatch sounds a bit frustrated.

"Yes, I can't go anywhere, I'm waiting for someone to tell me if the truck is going into the shop to get fixed or what is going to happen."

"*Kenworth is going to tow the truck to the shop in Springdale. Just wait there for the tow truck.*"

"I'll be here, I can't go anywhere. Is this going to be covered under warrantee?"

"*We don't know yet.*" They sound as confused about things as I am.

"Will someone let me know?"

"*Of course.*"

Click.

Wow, that was short and sweet. I don't like the way they handle things and I don't like being left in the dark. I'm not sure I can get used to this after all. I can't do anything about it right now so I'll just go along with whatever they are doing for now.

Miss Kitty seems agitated, does she feel the tension in the air? I need to stay calm about this for her sake if nothing else. She senses something is wrong.

***

It's been four and a half hours since I spoke to dispatch, the tow truck just arrived and both Miss Kitty and I have to ride in the tow truck with a driver who does not like having pets in his truck. He seems rather upset so I'm trying to stay far, far away while he is hooking everything up. Miss Kitty is throwing a fit about being in a carrier and I know she is going to be screaming all the way. Sigh. This is going to be fun. Not.

It was a very long ride to say the least. The driver barely said a word and Miss Kitty made up for it by expressing her discomfort every few minutes so we didn't forget. No radio, no talking and only the sound of Miss Kitty telling of her woes the entire trip.

Bad news, the truck is going to be down for at least three weeks. Dispatch offered a rental truck again. My biggest issues with the rental truck is that I have to pay a pet deposit of $1,000 as well as the rental fee of $700 a week on top of my truck payment of $975 per week and fuel. How is that a good option for me? They keep saying that at least it will keep me rolling. Rolling maybe but not making any money, I might actually be paying them to work. As if I'm not already doing that.

There is supposed to be a Freightliner at the yard if I want to switch trucks again. I'm really not sure what to do. I can't keep switching trucks all the time. I get charged a down payment as well as the repair fees for the previous truck and another pet deposit. I guess I can try one more time. Maybe I'll be better off with a Freightliner, maybe I won't have so many issues with it. Good thing I bought that little trailer, I'm going to need it to move all my things.

One last time, I told dispatch this was the last time I would do this. There are plenty of companies willing to hire me and I bet I can find one that has decent equipment. I don't mean to be disrespectful but this is trying my last nerve. I have to have a good truck if I want to make any money out here and all I seem to get from them are lemons. I wouldn't have stayed but they made it sound like I was just over reacting and things would work out if I just hung in there a little longer. Everything would be fine. I agreed to stay and try one last final time.

Lord, let this one work, please. I can't handle swapping trucks all the time and all the deposit fees. If it doesn't work, send me to the right company to work for. Thank you, Lord.

Chapter 41

THIS TRUCK IS A lot smaller than any Freightliner I have ever driven. We will make due, we have to. I had to leave a lot of things in the trailer but we have more than enough to get by out here. Here we go, we have a new truck and a load. Back to California again, of course. I'm hoping for the best. Miss Kitty isn't speaking to me right now. She is very upset about losing another truck and doesn't like this one at all.

California is sunny and warm which is such a relief from all the winter weather we have been driving in. I might just like California a little right now. The traffic is still a mess but I'll take that over the icy roads across the country. It's Spring but winter hasn't given up quite yet.

Miss Kitty enjoys coming out here, she loves all the smells and little critters. We watched a rabbit playing in the parking lot this morning. She wanted out so bad but I was afraid she would try to bring it on the truck as a pet. I've heard you can train them to use the litter box but I sure don't know how to train a rabbit. I don't think she would know what to do with one either. Can they jump onto the bed? Where would it sleep? They have to have special food and they like to hide so I don't think a truck would be a good place for a rabbit. Would they even allow one on the truck?

A load East, back West, one South and now North. Kind of, we are heading to Nevada. The weather is past warm and is downright hot, we have to keep the ac on most of the time. Isn't it supposed to get cooler the farther North we get? I think it's getting hotter. From Kingman up, the temperature has kept rising and now it's 110 degrees. The ac is working hard to keep it cool in here.

We have the pleasure of going through Las Vegas to get up to Reno. By pleasure I mean it is a pain in the tush. It's really pretty at night when everything is lit up. I love to drive by all the casinos and try to see what they have going on. I stop every now and then to eat at the buffets but today, in the daylight, it is not pretty and we don't have time to stop right now.

As we are going up highway 95, heading out of Las Vegas, the dash went out. By out I mean it is totally blank. Well, all the gauges on this truck are on the screen and without the screen working I can't see the speedometer, temperature or even the air pressure. There are no gauges what so ever anywhere else. How much fuel did I have? How fast am I going? I'm pulling a hill so how hot is the engine running?

I have to stop to call breakdown, I can't drive like this. Why is this happening to me? I have hometime scheduled next week for the big birthday bash week with the family, I can't miss that. Talk about rotten timing. I better make that call.

"Breakdown."

"Hey this is Tory; I need to know what to do when the dash goes out on the new Freightliners. Can you help me with that?"

"*No ma'am, you will have to take it into a shop and get it diagnosed, we don't have any way of telling what's going on with the new trucks without hooking it up to the computer.*"

"Would you happen to know where the nearest shop is located in route? I'm headed to Reno."

"*It shows the closest one to be in Las Vegas, you will have to turn around and go back, you can't drive it all the way to Reno like that.*"

Please Lord, don't let me be stuck in Las Vegas and miss going home for the birthday bash.

"Alright, send me the directions and I will head back down there."

"*Be careful driving it like that.*" Breakdown warns.

Click.

This better be a quick fix or I'm calling the family to come get us, we aren't that far from Colorado and I'll just leave the truck at the shop in Las Vegas for them to worry about. This is too much, none of the trucks I have gotten have been worth a darn. I can't do this; I have to have a truck that runs. I'm going to have to start looking for a different company, what choice do I have?

Thank goodness they were able to get right to me and run the diagnostics. They did an update and everything seems to be working fine. I need to get this load delivered so I can get a load back to see the family, I should be able to make it if nothing else goes wrong.

I spoke too soon, or maybe I cursed it or jinked it myself when I made that statement. Right before I reached the receiver, the dash went out again. I'm less than 30 miles from the Wal-Mart I'm delivering to; I'll go deliver the load and then head to the shop that's just a few miles farther down the road. This isn't funny anymore; I really can't afford to be shut down right now.

***

I made the delivery, called breakdown while I was being unloaded and now, I'm at the shop. I'm really hoping it will be as quick as last time. I'm heading in to talk to them now.

"*Can I help you?*" Said the receptionist at the desk.

"Hi, I'm Tory and I need someone to run a diagnostic on my truck. I need to get it fixed as soon as possible. Breakdown said they would call you and set it up for me."

"*I'm sorry ma'am, we are backed up and it will be at least 2 weeks before we can even get your truck in to see what the problem is.*" The salesman in a suit said as he walked out of his office.

"You can't even run the diagnostic? I just had it checked in Las Vegas, they did an update on it and it worked fine until just before I got here."

"*I'll try to get someone out to do the diagnostic but we won't be able to do anything about it for at least 2 weeks.*" Said the salesman in the suit.

"Alright, just send someone out so I at least know what the problem is, I'll try to find some place to get it fixed. Thank you."

This is so not good. Let's see if breakdown has any solutions.

***

Just wonderful, their solutions are to either wait till they get around to it while I stay in a motel here or I can fly home for my hometime and then just fly back and wait here in a motel until it's fixed. They said I can't drive it as is even to take it to another shop.

Dear Heavenly Father, please help this truck. I need to be home for the birthday bash, the kids count on it so much. They wait anxiously all year for gramma to get back to town for the big party time. Can you send one of your mechanic angels down to fix it please? I don't care what happens after my hometime but I really need to be there. Thank you, Lord.

The most amazing thing happened, I was asked to move the truck over to a different spot so they could get another truck in first and all of a sudden, the dash came back on. Everything is working. The shop guy said there wouldn't be anything they could do to the truck if everything was working so there was no use in me waiting there. Thank the good Lord, I'm heading home. I called dispatch and asked if they had a load headed there but they didn't so I asked permission to take the truck deadhead all the way and they agreed. It's 877 miles and that is going to cost me quite a bit but I don't care, I will be home in time for the birthday bash. That had to be God answering my prayer. Thank you, Lord. Thank you so very much and thank the angel who did the repair work for me.

Chapter 42

~~

WE HAD WATER BALLOONS, water guns, water slides and all kinds of water games. We did BBQs almost every single night and played board games till the kids fell asleep then watched a movie until the adults were falling asleep. I am beyond thankful that I didn't miss this time with the family, it was so great. Miss Kitty called a truce with the other kitties and everyone had a blast. This had to be one of the greatest birthday bashes ever. I wish it could last forever.

I got a load to Houston as soon as my hometime was up. No surprise, the truck started acting up again. I had prayed for it to be fixed for the birthday bash and it was but now that it's over, the truck is starting to breakdown again. From Houston I asked to go to Texarkana to get it fixed at the shop there so I could check the mail. It's not that far away so they agreed. Now I am sitting in Texarkana, at the shop, debating on what I want to do.

There is just no way I can stay with this company. My maintenance account is now in the negative over $6,000 and the truck is in the shop racking up more debt. I have barely been able to pay my bills. I am going to have to find a different company. I guess I have plenty of time to look, they informed me that I had to get a new ICU board and a relay switch. Everything is on back order all across the country so there is no telling how long that will take to get them in.

To top that off, this company just got bought out by another company. It's definitely time for me to find somewhere else to go. Where to start looking. I can't believe I am going through this again and even in the same city. Ugh!

***

I think Miss Kitty recognizes the smells here. We aren't at the old yard but she knows it smells familiar. She has been sitting up on the dash watching everything and looking all around. She is waiting to get out and play at the yard, I think. That is closed and locked up, we can't go back there.

I think I might have found a company to work for. Some of the people who used to work for the last company are now working for the son of the owner from the last company. The father died and the son has started a new company since the old one is gone. Their yard is just up the road in Ashdown. They said I can do my orientation online and just come in for one day to fill out all the final paperwork and do the drug test.

They don't have owner operators or lease purchase programs so I will be just a company driver. I think that sounds really good to me right now. No more truck payments, I won't have to pay for any repairs of the truck or trailer and I won't even have to buy my own fuel. I'm going for it. What do I have to lose? I've already lost almost everything.

I did all the orientation on the computer while I was sitting at the Freightliner shop. Everything is done except the drug test and the final paperwork. I can even move most of my things into a truck while I'm up there so all I will have to do is turn this one in in Tulsa, load whatever I have left on the truck into the car and drive back down here. I'll be ready to work the day I get back here.

***

As soon as we arrived at the yard in Ashdown, everyone came out to greet us and wanted a hug. Their first words were "Welcome home Tory" and I almost cried. They even told Miss Kitty how much they missed her but she wouldn't allow any hugs, she just sniffed everyone and purred. I think we found where we belong.

We talked to so many people we knew from the other company. Some of the drivers, one even took us out for lunch, and most of the office. Dispatch was thrilled we would be back on the board; we have a really good record and they remember how we like to run. They said they would have a load set up the minute they knew we would be ready to roll.

I just need to get the truck back up to Tulsa and turn it in so we can get back down here and get back to work. I'm really looking forward to working with everyone again. I have missed them. I passed the drug test and made sure all the paperwork was signed taken care of. The shop finally got the truck done so we are all set. I'm ready to get back to work.

Easier said than done, we did get the truck back to Tulsa. I checked in with the guard when I got here and told them I was just cleaning the truck out and would be leaving this company. They made notes in the computer and I got to work cleaning everything out and packing everything up.

As soon as they arrived in the office, they called me in for a random drug test. No problem, I went in and they said it was a centimeter shy of pee which equates to a refusal to pee which goes on my record as a positive drug test. What? No, I'll just retest. Nope, not allowed. What in the world is happening? This can't even be real, I must have fallen asleep and am having a nightmare. With a positive drug test, I can't drive for anyone at all period. I already have another job lined up, all I have to do is get down there.

I tried to argue, no luck there, I tried to reason with them, too late. They have an MRO – Medical Review Officer that I have to deal with and she sent me to see a urologist so I could get an ultrasound on my bladder. I had to pay for that out of my pocket. It came back fine so the MRO informed me she had gone ahead and entered a positive drug test on my permanent record with the drug testing clearing house. Say what? Absolutely not. How do I fight this?

Since I no longer work for the company, I can no longer communicate with them. The MRO has already entered in the results on the clearing-house so I can no longer speak with her. My only choice is to dispute it with the FMCSA – Federal Motor Carrier Safety Administration. They are the ruling organization over truckers who make and enforce the rules. Guess what? You cannot dispute a positive test result no matter what the reason. I have only one option left; I call an attorney. They accepted the case but after researching it further, they declined it.

Me and Miss Kitty are staying with friends in Okmulgee, since my cousin is in the process of moving, while I'm trying to figure everything out. They think this is ridiculous too, they want me to find a way to fight it. I have tried everything I know and I can't find a way to fight this. I did not test positive. The rules state that a positive test means you are restricted from operating any safety sensitive equipment. You have to go through a substance abuse program your license is suspended until you complete all the requirements and you are now considered a drug addict for the rest of your life.

I had to let the company that had just hired me know what was going on and they had no choice but to rescind their offer of employment. I won't be able to work for them or anyone else ever again. All over one centimeter of pee. It's as if a nuclear bomb just exploded in my life. This is all I know; I have been a truck driver for so long I don't even know if I can do anything else. Where do I go from here? Is this the end of my career?

My friends contacted a tv reporter who seemed interested in running a story on it but after I submitted all the information to her, she never got back in touch with me. This is it, the end of the line. There is nothing more I can do. There is no way to fight it or change it.

I can't drive truck, operate a forklift, haul anything in a company vehicle, drive a bus or taxi, not even door dash, grub hub, uber or any of them could hire me. So where does that leave me? Will I be able to get trained to do anything else while I basically have a drug charge on my record? All this because I was shy one centimeter of pee.

I need to rethink this. This is not the end; this is just a new beginning. Life is full of change and where one thing ends something better begins. I am looking forward to discovering what God's new plan for my life will be. He gives you more than what you have lost so I look forward to the blessings he has in store for us. I'm sure Miss Kitty will love her new house whatever that might be.

Dear Lord God, I don't understand what is happening or why but I trust that you have a plan in this and a purpose for all things. I believe this is just part of your plan for my life. If it is an end to one thing, it must be a beginning to something else. Whatever it might be, I trust you and look forward to what you have prepared for me now. Thank you, Lord. Amen.

CPSIA information can be obtained
at www.ICGtesting.com
Printed in the USA
BVHW050332130323
659895BV00020B/231